RODNEY PENFOLD, GENIUS

DICK CATE

WALKER BOOKS

AND SUBSIDIARIES

LONDON · BOSTON · SYDNEY

First published 1991 by Walker Books Ltd
87 Vauxhall Walk, London SE11 5HJ

This edition published 1998

2 4 6 8 10 9 7 5 3 1

Text © 1991 Dick Cate
Cover illustration © 1991 Paul Sample

Printed in England

Britsh Library Cataloguing in Publication Data
A catalogue record for this book is available
from the British Library.

ISBN 0-7445-6061-6

To Gina Pollinger

ONE

"Could I have a word, genius?"

I was already late for assembly that morning but naturally I stopped to see who wanted me.

It was Miss Quibble, our English teacher.

"I just wondered if your brilliant mind has had time to consider the proposition I put to you last night?" she said. "About the school mag?"

"I don't really think it's me, miss."

"I'm sure you'd be first rate, Rodney," said Miss Quibble as we headed hallwards. "In any case, didn't you tell me last week you were going to be a writer?"

"That was last week, miss," said Charlotte Bunting, catching up with us. (Charlotte really fancies me – and who can blame the girl?) "Rodney's in a different phase now."

"A different phase?" said Miss Quibble.

"He keeps going through these phases, miss," said Charlotte.

"Yeah!" said Lester, my little brother, drifting up like a piece of spare flotsam. "They usually last about two days!"

"And in what phase are we at the moment?" Miss Quibble asked.

"It's a secret, miss," I said.

"Miss, this week he's a detective," said Lester.

"A detective? I must say you don't *look* like a detective, Rodney."

"Correct, miss!" said Lester. "He doesn't look tough enough!"

"I wouldn't go that far," said Miss Quibble, "but I'm sure you'd get the school magazine off to a good start, Rodney. Come on – how about writing me a nice long story for the first edition?"

"What kind of a story, miss?" I asked her.

"Any kind of story," she said. "A detective story, if you like."

"Oh, he couldn't do that, miss," said Lester. "Particularly not a *detective* story!"

"Why ever not?"

"Because of our dad, miss. Rodney has this thing about—"

"I haven't, miss," I said. "It's just I wouldn't know where to start."

"If I were you, Rodney," said Miss Quibble with a smile, "I should start by going into assembly!"

TWO

Following her glance, I saw that Tarzan – our games master, Mr McGeorge – was standing at the hall doors waiting for us to go in.

"Don't rush yourself, Penfold," he growled at me through his fangs as we passed. "You're only keeping the Head waiting, that's all!"

The Head, Mr Battrey, is a tall stringy individual who rarely leaves his office and his beloved computers, and the moment I saw him on-stage I guessed we were in for another dollop of his one-and-only subject: the holy and sacred Image of the school.

"I think you all know Mrs Wright," he started, pausing just long enough for us to roll our eyes and feel ill. "Well, I'm afraid she has, once again, found cause to complain about our little community."

Mrs Wright lives just down the road from our school, in Park View Gardens. Her husband used to be some big shot on the council before he snuffed it at a banquet (probably over-eating). Most people were lucky enough to know Mrs Wright only as a shadowy figure spying from behind her net curtains.

Our family, unfortunately, knew her a little better than that. A corner of her back garden touched a corner of ours and she was forever moaning about the pong from our compost blowing over her fence. If it wasn't that, it was our beech tree deliberately dropping its leaves on her lawn.

Last week she'd complained about a girl from our school dropping litter – again deliberately – in her front garden. Which was a ridiculous suggestion because the kids from our school would never do a thing like that: they'd just drop it anywhere. The local rag had carried the headline, SCHOOL GIRL DELIBERATELY DROPS LITTER IN EX-COUNCILLOR'S FRONT GARDEN – and you can imagine how pleased the Head had been about that.

"It now appears that Mrs Wright's dog has been stolen," he went on, "and she is naturally very worried."

That I could imagine. Because although Mrs Wright seemed devoid of all other feelings, she did appear to be fond of her dog, a bumptious old Pekinese called Pagan.

"Once more Mrs Wright seems to think a child from our school is involved," Mr Battrey was saying, "though what motive anyone could have for stealing such a dog, I cannot comprehend."

Of course, at the word "motive" my detective-type brain swept into action: motives are terribly important things for us detectives. *Why should anyone want to steal Mrs*

Wright's Pagan? I asked myself. Was it possibly to construct a fur coat for an undersized Eskimo? Or was the council using poor dead Pagan to replace a worn-out brush on their new-fangled gutter sweeper?

"So if anybody can help," droned Mr Battrey, "I would be obliged if you'd let me know. And, for your information, Mrs Wright's dog is a mongrel – large, long-haired, and black and white."

You can imagine how amazed I was. I mean, we all knew Mr Battrey was vague on names, but now he seemed to be confusing his canines as well.

"It isn't, sir," I said, putting my hand up. "It's brown." I paused long enough for everyone to drink in my brilliance. "And, sir, it isn't exactly large, sir, because it's a Pekinese!"

"Thank you, Richard," he said (you see my point about names?), "but I think we can safely assume Mrs Wright knows what kind of dog she's got, don't you?" I heard some of the ignorant bunch behind me – mainly the soccer team thugs – titter.

"And now," he said, "an entirely different subject, but the waterproof compass from Miss Airey's Space Exhibition appears to have disappeared. I *would* like that returned immediately. Understood? Mr McGeorge, would you take over?"

Tarzan grunted and swaggered towards the

front, and a moment later Mr Battrey had stalked off-stage and back into his computer room, no doubt to plug himself in.

THREE

Can anybody tell me what you'd do with a waterproof compass in space?

Personally, I cannot imagine.

I mean, there's no water up there, is there?

And is there a north or south? An up or a down? I don't think so.

I've always imagined that floating about in space must be like being at my old junior school. We had non-competitive games and vertical streaming and no one knew where they were (especially not the teachers).

Another weird thing about my old junior school was a kid called Corvel, whose chief delight was to terrorize all the little kids, and yours truly in particular. I hadn't seen him for yonks – not since we'd moved – but last week he'd turned up again like an old familiar nightmare.

At my last school all the teachers thought he was ace. I'll never forget he was chosen to play the angel Gabriel in our nativity play because he looked so good and kind; I always thought he looked especially good and kind when he was torturing you to death in the bogs.

And it was the same at this school. All the

teachers liked him; and he was already up to his nasty tricks.

Passing Miss Airey's classroom that morning, I'd noticed Corvel giving the eye to the waterproof compass. What's more, I happened to know that he'd seen the film on TV the week before in which a crook had wrapped up a pistol in a plastic bag, then secreted it in the cistern of a bog. I'd heard Corvel talking about it with Byrne, his side-kick, during one of his torture-the-little-kids sessions in the school bogs.

And putting the two facts together, I knew who had stolen Miss Airey's missing compass.

And where he'd hidden it.

So at breaktime, as soon as I saw that Corvel and Byrne were safely engaged in the yard, shaking sweets out of first years, I nipped indoors and headed for the bogs.

Outside the bogs there's a notice-board, and Desmond Fiely was squinting up at it. Normally I feel sorry for Desmond Fiely, and not only because he's in the same class as my brother. His eyes are too close together so that he looks like a guinea-pig with specs on. He has a big mouth, Desmond, and a lot of silly people – including my especially silly brother – think he knows everything; but in fact he's pretty thick and the only thing he knows about is computers. I tried to smile at him as I went past, and he gave me a sickly smile back, and seemed to shake his head, which I didn't think anything of at the time.

The bogs were empty so I bombed into the first cubicle. Standing on the seat, it was easy for me to reach my hand into the cistern. Easy, but not nice: the water was cold and slimy... And that wasn't the worst part. I kept imagining *something* in the water – a giant water rat or something – about to grab my hand and haul me down into the depths.

I was standing on the bog seat thinking how brave and fearless I was when all of a sudden a voice behind me said, "Good morning, Rodney. So this is your latest consuming passion, is it? Climbing on toilet seats? Sure you don't need a rope?"

It was Mr Toogood, our history teacher. Everybody likes him because he's always cracking last century's jokes and isn't a slave-driver like the other teachers. At the time, rumour had it he was trying for the vacant deputy head's post, but everybody knew Tarzan would get it – because he had much bigger gym-shoes.

"The last time we had converse, Rodney," Mr Toogood said, "you gave me to understand you were hoping to be the next Astronomer Royal."

"I was star-struck at the time, sir," I said.

"Are we to understand you've climbed up

there to obtain a better view of the stars? Or have you now decided to take up plumbing?"

"Not exactly, sir."

"What exactly *are* you doing, Rodney, if that's not a rude question?"

"Trying to get the water to run, sir."

"I take it you've tried pulling the chain?"

"I never thought of that, sir," I said.

I pulled the chain, trying not to work it, but you know what Life is like. Normally if you pull our school chains you can rely on them *not* to work. They just make a *clonk* that signals your embarrassing position to the rest of the known universe. But not this time.

"Well done, Rodney," said Mr Toogood. "Now outside into that thing called a playground and have some lovely fresh air, like a normal healthy boy!"

"Just wash my hands first, sir," I said.

"Very well. Then straight outside," he said as he went.

I washed my hands. There was no soap: I think people have it for breakfast in our school, then eat the paper towels for afters. I waited until I heard Mr Toogood trumpeting in the yard, then nipped into the second cubicle to finish off my job.

But it would have been a lot better for me if I'd followed his advice.

FOUR

This time I shut the door behind me, but it didn't do me a lot of good. I was just trying lucky dip number two when Corvel came into the bogs, Byrne just behind him, and said, "What you doing in there, Rodney?"

At my old junior school I often had the creepy notion that Corvel knew exactly what was going through my mind. I used to offer him my sweets before he even asked because I was convinced he already knew I had them. And I had that feeling now as I wondered how he could see me through the cubicle door (not to mention all the grafitti on it).

"Nothing, Eric," I said.

"Get out here!" he said.

While I dried my hand on the back of my trousers so he wouldn't know what I'd been up to, I was thinking, *My God! What if I'd found the compass in one of the cisterns? What if it were actually in my pocket right now? What a lucky thing it is I haven't found it.*

I must have looked like one of the walking dead when I came out. Although I was actually bigger than Corvel, he managed to turn my blood to ice.

"What's the matter with you, Rodney?" he asked.

"Nothing, Eric," I said. "Just been on the bog. It's the prunes."

Byrne laughed like a blocked drain.

"What prunes?" asked Corvel.

"My mum made me eat prunes this morning," I explained.

Which was almost true. My mum is a firm believer in what she calls the Natural Way which – to put it shortly – means everybody in our family is force-fed on dried fruit and normally has the galloping trots.

"What you looking like that for?" Corvel asked. "Something up?"

He looked at me with his innocent blue eyes and I strove to remember a book of my dad's called *How to Stay Sane in a Crazy World* by Hiram K. Blott or Klott or Heimelburger. Chapter One states quite categorically: "Nobody can see into your mind. Your mind is a private world, belonging only to you." I thought, *What a wonderful thing literature is, sometimes* – and I said to Corvel, "It's only the prunes."

"You been up to something?"

"Nothing, Corvy. Honest."

"Why are you so white?" He looked past me into the cubicle. "You hidden something in that cistern?"

"No, Corvy."

"Get up there and fish it out."

I got back on the seat and dipped my hand back in the slime. You can imagine what I was thinking: *My God! What if it's actually in there?*

"There's nothing there, Corvy. I wouldn't tell you a lie."

"I hope not, Rodney. That would be naughty."

"You want me to look?" Byrne asked him.

Corvel nodded.

Byrne shoved me aside and dipped his big paw in the cistern.

"Nothing," he said. He stepped down and wiped his paw on my blazer. "Thanks awfully, Rodney," he said, and burped in my face.

I could see Corvel was far from satisfied.

Nobody can see into your mind, I told myself. Followed by *God bless Professor Blott, Klott, or Heimelburger.*

"I do hope you're not telling me lies, Rodney," he said.

"I'm not, Eric."

"We're still pals, aren't we?"

"Sure we are, Eric."

Corvel smiled at me.

A small kid came in, unzipping urgently as he walked. He was the smallest kid of the new intake, a real squit.

"What d'you think you're doing?" Corvel asked him. The Squit didn't answer, just stopped in his tracks and went white. I remembered how Corvel used to stop us going to the toilet at break so he could have the fun of seeing us do it in our pants.

"Get in that cubicle and stop there till I tell you," he said.

"OK, Eric," said the Squit.

He went in the first cubicle and shut the door behind him.

"And don't pee till I tell you!" said Corvel.

Byrne laughed. I'd liked to have done something. But what can you do?

"So what you up to?" Corvel asked me.

"Nothing, Eric. Honest."

"You see that film the other night?"

"What film?"

He looked so disappointed in me that I wondered if Professor Blott, Klott, or Heimelburger, was wrong after all. *Nobody*, I kept telling myself.

"You got any money on you?"

I shook my head. I gave him a packet of mints. I hate mints. Besides, Oscar, this hound dog we are cursed with, had left his horrible rabid teethmarks on the packet.

"Thanks, Rodney. You sure you've got no money?"

"Sorry, Eric," I said.

"Lift your arms up."

He frisked me.

"You sure you've got nothing?"

"Absolutely," I said. *Nobody!* I kept thinking.

I did have some money, actually. It was taped to the inside of my ankle. I got that idea from one of my dad's books. Corvel doesn't read books. He just tears them up.

"Absolutely!" he said, copying the way I talked. "What d'you know about this compass?"

"What compass?"

"Don't mess about, Rodney. It isn't nice." He put his arm round my shoulders and squeezed me. "We're pals, aren't we?"

"Ask him about the dog," said Byrne.

"You know anything about this missing dog, Rodney?" Corvel asked me.

"No, Eric."

"If you do hear anything about it," he said, "I want to know first. You got that? And if there's any money, we want it."

"Like with the other dog, eh, Corvy!" laughed Byrne.

"Shut your big mouth!" Corvel told him.

Just then another first year kid came in. West Indian. This, though I didn't know it at the time, was the world famous boxer, Hamilton the Third, future tiddlywink-weight champion of the world.

But Corvel knew him all right.

"Well, well, well! Everything comes to them that wait!" he said, smiling as Hamilton the

Third stepped up to the urinal. "Aren't you the kid I told to report to me yesterday afternoon?"

"So what, man?" said Hamilton, half turning round from what he was doing. "I don't take no orders from nobody!"

Corvel smiled. He nodded at me. "You better go, Rodney," he said. "You won't want to watch this. Might make you puke up your prunes!"

Byrne laughed like a dutiful half-witted seal.

"OK, Eric," I said.

And I got out as fast as I could.

FIVE

You think I should have stayed behind and helped the two first years? That I should have powed Byrne through the wall and flushed Corvel down the toilet? You're so right. Only Life isn't like that, is it?

You might also think all that garbage Corvel had spouted about the compass might have put me off the idea that he had nicked it himself; but there again you would be wrong.

Because I knew what Corvel was like.

The same applied to Mrs Wright's dog. The fact that he'd asked me to look out for it only convinced me he already had it.

Also, there was the business of "the other dog" – the one Byrne had mentioned. *What other dog?* I wondered. *And why had Byrne mentioned money? And did that mean they'd nicked another dog and sold it to somebody? Or had they got some other way of making money?*

All morning I devoted my brilliant mind to these and other questions and by dinner time I had it all figured. *And* I knew what we were going to do about it.

"Let me get this straight, Rodney," said

Charlotte as we wrestled with our vegeburgers. "You now think Corvel has nicked not only Mrs Wright's dog, but another dog as well?"

"Not to mention Miss Airey's waterproof compass!" sniggered Lester.

"Is that what you really think, Rodney?" asked Charlotte.

"I don't think, Charlotte," I said. "I *know*."

"Boy, oh, boy!" said Lester.

"Shut your trap, Lester!" I said.

"I'll tell you who's got Mrs Wright's dog," he said. "That tramp."

"Tramp?" I said. "What tramp?"

"The one we saw on Saturday night."

It was true we'd seen a scruffy bloke in jeans and an old overcoat knocking on Mrs Wright's door at the weekend: probably just a wino, begging. He had a big black beard.

"Tramps don't do that sort of thing, Lester," I said, "not in real life. That sort of thing only happens in books."

"Tell you what," he said, "why don't we call ourselves The Secret Seven? When I was a kid I read a book called that."

"Let's face it, Lester," I said, spearing his last chip, "you *are* a kid. Besides, there's only one slight snag. How can we call ourselves The Secret Seven when there're only three of us?"

"We could expand," he said. "We could put an advert in the paper. Secret society requires new members! We could include Oscar."

I am *not* having that stupid dog in my gang!" I said.

"Don't go on, you two," said Charlotte. "And, Rodney, if Corvel has nicked Mrs Wright's dog, why should he suggest that you've got it? It doesn't make sense."

"You should have seen his face," I said.

"I still think it's the tramp who's got Pagan," said my little brother. "And I *know* you're wrong about the compass."

"Oh yeah? How come?" I asked.

"Because Harriet Farlaughn had it after you saw Corvel looking at it."

"Harriet Farlaughn?" I said sceptically.

You know Desmond Fiely, the kid who was looking at the notice-board outside the bogs? Well, Harriet Farlaughn is his girlfriend and they're well-matched because they're both spaced out. She's crazy about animals, and a real doze. She'd forget her head if it wasn't screwed on tight.

"When exactly was Harriet Farlaughn supposed to have had the compass?" I asked.

"After registration. Desmond saw her with it just before she went to feed the hamster. It's her turn this week."

"Poor thing!" I said. "Has it died of starvation yet?"

"It's no good arguing, you two," said Charlotte. "That won't get the dog – or dogs – back, will it? Question is, what are we going to do?"

"We're going to go round to Mrs Wright's," I said. "Tonight. To start our inquiries."

Just then Miss Quibble drifted up to our table.

"Well, genius?" she said.

"Too late, miss," said Charlotte. "Rodney's just started his first case."

"He's crazy, miss," said my little brother. "He just can't help it."

"Oh dear! Then I shall just have to look elsewhere for a writer. The name Arnold Rattner comes to mind. Or Isobel Plunk."

"They sound ideal, miss," I said. "Did you pick them out of a hat?"

Miss Quibble rummaged in her handbag. "I don't suppose I can persuade you with these, Rodney?" She held out a tube of mints.

I stared in horror. It wasn't so much that I hated mints, but these mints were special: Oscar's teeth marks were still embedded in them.

"That new boy, Eric Corvel, has just given them to me," said Miss Quibble. "He's such a nice boy – don't you think, Rodney?"

SIX

Have you ever noticed how people grow to resemble their dogs?

When Mrs Wright opened her front door we saw her bulgy-eyed face looking down at us and, from the region of her ankles, an almost identical face (though perhaps slightly hairier) glaring up.

"So you've got your dog back again, Mrs Wright?" I said.

She glanced down at the Peke for a moment.

"Oh, it's not Pagan who's lost. I couldn't do that to my own little boy, could I, my precious?"

Pagan yapped his assent.

"We heard you'd lost a dog," Charlotte said above the noise, "and we wondered if we could help."

"Quiet, Pagan, you naughty boy!" said Mrs Wright, and the Peke, recognizing the leader of his pack, quietened at once. "I suppose you'd better come in. But do wipe your feet."

As she closed the door, I noticed on the wall behind her a photograph of her husband holding up some medal he'd just been presented with – probably for smugness.

"So whose dog is it that's lost, Mrs Wright?" I asked as we went down the passage towards the kitchen. Pagan, waggling his tail, led the way like a Japanese standard bearer.

"My niece's. She works for the BBC, you know."

"That must be nice," said Charlotte. "What does she do?"

"I couldn't really tell you," said Mrs Wright, "but it's something important."

"What's her name?" asked Charlotte.

"Sally Bright."

It didn't ring a bell.

We were in the kitchen now, one of those fitted affairs, probably hacked out of the Brazilian rain forest (my mother would have had a fit). Mrs Wright sat down at the table and cut herself a large piece of fruit cake.

"Sally's coming back to collect the dog on Friday, so I must have it by then."

"Is she very fond of it?" Charlotte asked.

"Oh, yes. Very."

Mrs Wright broke off a piece of fruit cake and gave it to Pagan.

"The other dog was black and white, was it?" I asked.

"That's right. One of those big woolly creatures. Of absolutely no real value, of course. Not a pedigree, or anything like that."

"Was it friendly?" Charlotte asked.

"Friendly? My dear, it wouldn't leave poor Pagan alone, and my little baby doesn't like being fussed over, do you, my precious?"

Pagan said he didn't, and his mummy gave him another piece of cake.

"What was its name?" I asked.

"Name? Bess, I believe. Something like that."

"Was it taken from the house, Mrs Wright?"

"Oh no, dear. I couldn't do with it in the house. I tried, but it kept sniffing poor Pagan and naturally my little boy didn't like that." She gave her little boy another piece of cake as a consolation prize. "I was afraid for my ornaments," she said, "it had such a swishy tail."

"Has anybody suspicious called lately?" asked Lester.

She thought for a moment, then said, "No."

"Not, for instance, on Saturday?"

"Definitely not," she said. "I would have remembered."

I was puzzled. Had she already forgotten about the tramp?

"So the dog was taken from outside, was it?" asked Charlotte.

"That's right, dear. I made a nice place for it."

"Could we see?" I asked.

"You children nowadays!" she said. "If you must. Just open the kitchen door and look right down at the bottom of the steps."

I undid the bolt and opened the back door. We went down the steps that led to the garden level. From there a second flight led to the basement door. We went down again. At the bottom of these steps there was a cardboard box with a sawn-off mattress inside it, still sopping wet from the downpour we'd had at the weekend.

"I thought it would be sheltered from the rain down there," called Mrs Wright from above, and Pagan poked his nose through the railings.

I came back up the steps and went round to the side of the house to inspect the gate there. It was bolted top and bottom.

"I suppose you unbolt this gate when you put out the dustbin?" I asked as I came back round to the garden.

"I never put it out, dear," Mrs Wright said. "My arm won't allow me. I just unbolt it and the men take it out for me. I know they're not supposed to, but they're very kind. I give them fifty pence every Christmas."

"They come on Thursdays, don't they?"

"When they're not on strike, they do. The government should do something about it."

"And when did your niece's dog vanish, Mrs Wright?" asked Charlotte.

"Saturday night, as far as I know, dear. I *think* I fed it on Saturday. It definitely wasn't there at Sunday teatime."

"And the side gate was locked, then?" I asked.

"I always do it straight after the bin men have gone. You can't trust anybody nowadays.

I think I'll go in. It's turning rather chilly."

Mrs Wright and her little boy retreated to the warmth of the kitchen and Charlotte and Lester climbed the steps to join them.

I walked down to the bottom of the garden. The side fencing was about two metres high. Even a big dog would need springy legs to leap over that. But at the bottom of the garden any dog could have negotiated the low rail and shrubs and then got into the Middletons' garden opposite – or the garden of number eleven, next to that on the left – or even our garden, to the right of it.

From where I stood I could see the light on in my dad's room. No doubt he would be up there, hatching out another of his dark plots. All this would be child's play to him. Crime, in a manner of speaking, was my dad's business. Which gave me one more reason for solving this case.

"I suppose your niece's dog could have got free itself and jumped over into one of the other gardens," I said when I rejoined the rest of them in the kitchen.

"Oh no, it couldn't possibly," said Mrs Wright. "Somebody must have untied it. I always looped its lead through the railings. It couldn't have escaped. It was definitely fastened up. The girl saw that."

"Which girl?" said Charlotte.

"Didn't I tell you? The girl who came round

31

on Friday night. She went down to see it, even though the rain had just started."

"But that wasn't the night it went missing?" I asked.

"No. In any case, it couldn't possibly have been her. She was such a nice girl. Lovely blonde hair and blue eyes. A Girl Guide. Not at all the sort of girl who would steal things. Very well-spoken. And shy. And very fond of animals. Pagan liked her, didn't you, my precious, and animals know about these things. She stayed out there in the rain talking to that other dog for ages."

I'm not a great fan of Girl Guides, to be honest. Ever since I emerged from my Naval Officer phase in my first term at nursery school I've had a thing against uniforms. But without knowing who she was, I was already beginning to like this particular Girl Guide. I could understand her feeling sorry for that dog soaking up rain at the bottom of the basement steps.

I wondered where it was now, and if Corvel had it. I wondered why he'd taken it in the first place. I'm not a great fan of dogs, either, though I know they're not all as useless as Oscar. But at least I'm one stage better than Corvel, who hates everything that breathes.

"Are you offering a reward for this dog, Mrs Wright?" I asked.

"Oh no," she said, looking uncomfortable.

"I couldn't afford that. I'm only a pensioner, you know."

"What was this girl's name, Mrs Wright?" asked Charlotte.

"I don't know, dear. She didn't say."

"Do you think she's at our school?" asked Lester.

"Probably. I don't know. Have you finished your questions? I usually watch the news at six o'clock."

We followed her out of the kitchen and down the passage, Pagan leading the way again. Before we reached the door, she went in the front room and drew the curtains.

"Good heavens!" she said, looking down into her front garden. She tapped on the window. "Shoo! You horrible child!"

"What is it, Mrs Wright?"

"It's that horrible child again! Dumping litter in my garden. Come and look."

I couldn't have been more surprised if I'd seen ET down there. It was Harriet Far-laughn – Desmond Fiely's girlfriend. She looked up at us, a mixture of shame and fear on her face, then scuttered away.

"Do you know her?" asked Mrs Wright. "Is she a friend of yours?"

"Never seen her before in our lives," I said.

I couldn't understand why Harriet Far-laughn would do a thing like that. She wasn't that kind of kid. I wondered why she was doing it. Then, looking further along the road, I saw Corvel and Byrne standing under a street lamp.

"Those big boys, Mrs Wright," I said. "Have you seen them before?"

As I spoke, Corvel seemed to look straight at me, and the thought occurred that if he could see through bog doors, then net curtains presumably would be no problem. I hastily stepped back from the window.

"No, I don't think so," she said.

"Do you mind if we go out the back way, Mrs Wright? To our house."

"Why? It's rather a nuisance. I don't want to miss the News."

"Please, Mrs Wright?" I said. "It is urgent."

SEVEN

"That proves it!" I said when we were safely in our garden shed with the door shut behind us.

"Proves what, Rodney?" said Charlotte.

"That Corvel nicked the dog," I said.

I reached up to the shelf and groped for the candle and matches wrapped in oiled canvas. I'd put them there during my Last Human Survivor on Earth phase, many moons ago.

"As far as I can see, it doesn't prove a thing," said Lester.

"You *wouldn't* see!" I said.

"Lester's right, Rodney," said Charlotte.

"Not *completely* proves it," I admitted, "but nine-tenths does."

The oiled canvas seemed to have worked brilliantly: it took only seventeen matches to light the candle.

"Let there be light!" I said.

Charlotte looked at me, her eyes soft with admiration. Girls do so love a practical man.

"Talking about lights," said Lester, "did you notice the light on in number eleven as we crossed the gardens just now?"

"Number eleven?" I said as I sat down on a bag of moss-killer, hoping it wouldn't damage my health. "Number eleven has been empty for yonks, Lester. What are you on about?"

"There's a light on in number eleven. I saw it as we left Mrs Wright's."

"*I* didn't see it, Lester," said Charlotte.

"It was in the kitchen," he said. "Sort of flickering."

"Lester," I said, "this may come as a shock to you but people round here do not congregate in the kitchens of empty houses with flickering lights. Not even tramps with black beards! Can we get down to business?"

"To be honest, Rodney," said Charlotte, "I still don't see how any of this proves Corvel stole the dog."

"Why else was he hanging around?" I said.

"That's probably something to do with Harriet," said Lester.

"Maybe," I admitted. "But I still bet you Corvel has the dog."

"But how did he get it?" asked Charlotte.

"He climbs over the gate one night, unbolts it, takes the dog and hands it out to Byrne, rebolts the gate, then climbs back over."

"But why should he bother to do that?" asked Charlotte. "Why should Corvel bolt the gate and climb over? Why didn't he just walk out with the dog and leave the gate open behind him?"

"He rebolted the gate and climbed over to

make it look like somebody had taken the dog over the back garden way," I said.

"But why should he do that?" asked Charlotte.

"To incriminate somebody else."

"Like who, for instance?" said Charlotte.

"Like somebody whose garden backs on to Mrs Wright's," I said.

"You mean you, Rodney?"

"Why not?" I said. "The guy hates me."

"Boy, oh, boy!" said Lester. "He hates everybody, you gump!"

"That's true," said Charlotte.

"There's a word for what you've got, Rodney," said Lester. "It's called pyromania."

He's always coming out with big words, my little brother, but he's not as red hot on them as he imagines.

"In any case," he said, "I've just thought of something. How come Corvel knew the dog was there in the first place? Can he see through walls nowadays? Has he got X-ray eyes all of a sudden?"

"He could have," I said. "That guy's real spooky." And I explained about Corvel seeing me through the bog door.

My brother just made one of his horrible chortles and said, "Didn't you tell me Desmond was at the notice-board? He's been acting as lookout for Corvel ever since last week. I thought everybody knew that."

"Even I did, Rodney," said Charlotte. "It's something to do with Harriet, isn't it, Lester?"

"Yeah. She's scared to death of Corvel."

"In any case it doesn't matter," I said. "Corvel knew about the dog because he'd been in the house."

"If he'd been in the house, why did Mrs Wright say she'd never set eyes on him before?" asked Lester.

"Because he was disguised," I said. "Don't you get it? Remember what Mrs Wright said about the Girl Guide? Fair hair. Blue eyes. Good looking."

"This I do not believe!" said Lester.

"Are you trying to say what I think you're trying to say, Rodney?" said Charlotte.

But I never answered that question.

Because we all heard a twig snapping just outside the shed door.

I waited long enough for whoever it was to crash through our hedge and across the Middletons' garden, before I shoved open the door and bravely rocketed out to stand sniffing the air as if eager for action.

"See anything?" said Charlotte.

"Unfortunately not!" I said.

"You should have moved faster!" said my brother. "You were scared!"

"Me?" I said. "Scared?"

Paralysed with fear is more the expression I

would have used: to be perfectly frank, Rodney is no hero.

"Why are we standing here?" said Charlotte. "Shall we investigate?"

"I was just thinking the same thing," I said.

We climbed through the hedge. The Middletons were not deeply into gardening and the grass on their lawn was so long that it was easy to see where someone had run straight across it. My heart sank when I saw this because I'd had enough excitement to last me a fortnight.

"What are we waiting for?" asked Charlotte.

"Thought I heard something," I said.

"Get on with it!" said my little brother.

I took my time crossing the Middletons' lawn. I guessed Corvel might leave Byrne behind to fight a rearguard action. When I reached the other side I poked my nose through the hedge extremely tentatively.

The grass of number eleven was so long I wouldn't have been surprised to see whole herds of buffalo grazing contentedly. But there was only a wide trail of footsteps leading to the far side of the house.

"I told you there was somebody in there!" said my little brother; he can be unbelievably petty about these things.

"It could be Corvel and Byrne," I said.

"You really are mad, Rodney!" he said. "It isn't them at all!"

"Anyhow, there's no light there now," I said.

"There was before."

"Most probably a reflection from the houses opposite," I said.

We stepped out of the hedge and stood for a moment in the dark. With each step away from our garden I felt less safe. I was just wondering if Corvel had got safely away by now, when Lester whispered, "Look! There *is* a light!"

I had to admit he was right. *And* it was flickering. My only consolation was that it wasn't in the kitchen, but in the basement.

"Shall we go and have a look?" said Charlotte.

She says the craziest things sometimes.

"Good idea!" I said.

We moved forward slowly – it's always me who has to be in the lead on these occasions – and as we approached the house we began to hear the sounds, at first indistinct, of somebody singing:

All things bright and beautiful,
All creatures great and small . . .

"Look!" said Lester when we got closer.

He was pointing at the basement window. The glass was none too clear but we were able to see inside. I could hardly believe it. A big black beard. I couldn't be absolutely sure but it *could* have been the tramp – the one we'd seen going into Mrs Wright's. At that moment he looked up and seemed to see us.

"That you?" he said. "Are you there? Hello?"

And we all ran like stink.

EIGHT

I didn't sleep much that night. I kept thinking about Corvel and what I'd said in the garden shed. I should never have got mixed up with the detective business in the first place. "A growing boy needs a full stomach!" my mother kept nagging all through breakfast, but to be honest, my impression was that I didn't have any stomach left at all.

I began to feel chirpier at school when I went into the yard and Corvel hardly bothered to glance in my direction. I began to think my little brother was right for once and it *hadn't* been Corvel outside the shed. Maybe he hadn't even seen me behind Mrs Wright's curtains. Maybe I'd just imagined these things.

All this strain, however, was having a disastrous effect on my bladder and I nipped round the back of the school and into the bogs. I was standing at the urinal feeling good and relaxed, thinking what a Silly Billy I'd been, and sniffing the relatively clean air that came through the window, when guess who stepped up alongside me.

"Thought I'd join you in a quick one, Rodney," he said as he unzipped and stared at the wall. "You doing me any favours today?"

"What d'you mean, Eric?" I said. "I haven't got any more sweets."

"Never mentioned sweets," he said.

He turned and smiled at me. I think that's the worst thing about Corvel: the way he smiles when he's about to do something horrible.

"I haven't got any money, Eric, if that's what you mean," I said. "I'd give you it if I had. Honest to God."

I stepped down and turned to go.

Byrne blocked my way.

"Who told you to move, Rodney?" said Corvel. "I haven't finished with you yet. I asked you a question. You got anything for me?"

"What you mean?" I said.

"You round the old lady's last night?"

"What old lady's?"

The expression in the pale blue eyes changed slightly, that was all.

"I hate people who lie to me, Rodney," he said.

Byrne, behind me, laughed.

"Oh, Mrs Wright, you mean!" I said. "Just making inquiries."

"What about? Her dog? What she tell you?"

"Only how it was nicked. It was fastened to the railings out the back. We're trying to find out where it is."

"She give you any money?"

"No."

He smiled. I remembered when he had first appeared in the nativity play, mothers had wept, and even some of the teachers had gone misty-eyed. I wished somebody would gallop to my rescue, but they never do, not in real life. That only happens in stories.

"Sorry about this, Rodney," he said, shaking his head and smiling like a saint, "but I just don't believe you. Get in that cubicle!"

He gave me a push.

Byrne started giggling.

"Get in there!" he said, pushing me again.

"What for, Corvy?"

"Never mind what for!"

The pair of them shoved me right in. There was a horrible stink.

"Some dirty person hasn't pulled the chain!" sniggered Byrne.

"What a shame!" said Corvel, smiling.

My throat had gone very dry.

Corvel smiled at me. Byrne was making the strange noises that no doubt his ancestors had made when they were still in the jungle, last week.

"I'm waiting, Rodney," Corvel said.

Just then the toilet door banged open and a voice said, "Corvy? That you in there?"

It was my little brother.

"What d'you want?" said Corvel.

"I thought I'd just let you know that Tarzan's on the prowl."

Corvel hesitated a second, then Byrne opened the door for him.

"Want one of these?" my brother said, holding out his Bubbly Bomb. "I don't like them, myself."

I was amazed. Grandma Hart, who is the only one in our family with any feelings, had brought us one each last night, and I knew Lester was particularly fond of them. If he'd had any sense, he'd have strapped his to the inside of his sock, as I had done with mine when he wasn't looking.

Corvel looked at him a moment, then took the Bubbly Bomb and shoved it in his mouth. He looked so pleased, so grateful, almost, that I wondered if perhaps even people like Corvel needed to be loved (though personally, I'd have been more delighted if it had been a real bomb he'd just stuffed in his mouth).

"You got one of these?" he asked, his eyes swivelling back to me.

"He ate his," my brother said. "I saw him."

Did I mention what an awful liar my little brother is?

"You're a fat greedy pig!" Corvel said. "What are you?"

"A fat greedy pig, Eric," I said.

Byrne laughed and pushed me so hard I almost fell down the bog.

"Where d'you go last night?" Corvel asked my brother.

"Round Mrs Wright's, you mean?"

"What d'you find out?"

"About the dog? Nothing. It was fastened to the basement railings when it was pinched, that's all. Me and Rodney are trying to find it."

"She offer you a reward?"

"Not yet. But we should screw something out of her in the end."

Corvel looked approvingly at my brother. "You got brains, you," he said. Then, glancing at me, "If you do find that dog and the old lady shells out, I want that money, Rodney. Don't forget!"

When they'd gone, I said, "Lucky thing you came in then."

"Not lucky at all," Lester said. "I heard you screaming."

You've probably noticed how he exaggerates all the time.

"How did you know what was going on?" I asked him.

"I saw him follow you. I climbed on the dustbins just outside the window so I could hear. I only just avoided being mangled to death in the council crusher."

"Pity," I said.

Just then Mr Toogood came in.

"You again, Rodney?" he said. "Not living here permanently, I hope? Pull that chain, will you? That's better. Everything all right?"

I told you what a dream he was. Everybody

46

liked him, but I couldn't see him making deputy head, not in our school. He was the sort of teacher who would deliberately step aside to avoid trampling on a kid.

"Only I got a message," he said. He went along the row of cubicles pushing back the doors. "Nobody's been bullying you two?"

"No, sir. Honestly."

"Only I have an idea a certain person is getting away with murder in this school, boys. I'd love to catch him. Love to. But it's very difficult, if you know what I mean. You haven't noticed anything furtive going on, have you, Rodney? Miss Quibble was telling me you'd joined the detective business this week."

"We don't know anything about bullying, sir," said Lester.

"Don't you, really?"

"No, sir."

When Mr Toogood had gone, I said, "Why did you tell him that?"

"Because it's not time yet," said Lester.

"Not time? What you on about?"

"We're going to wait till we've really got him."

"Got who?" I said.

"Corvel. We're going to fix him."

"We?" I said. "Who? When?"

He didn't answer, just looked at me.

"You know what?" I said. "You must be crazy. But anyhow thanks for giving up your

Bubbly Bomb. I'll pay you back one day."

"You can do it now," he said.

"How do you mean?"

"You can give me yours instead. It's taped to the inside of your sock. I saw you do it this morning."

NINE

That was the day the new girl arrived.

I was just coming back into the front yard – battling my way through the crisp packets and noticing out of the corner of my eye Corvel chewing happily on my brother's Bubbly Bomb (and my brother, round a corner, chewing happily on mine), when I saw this car come sliding along Park View Gardens.

It kept sliding a long time. A long, long time. Making a deep rich purring sound all the way.

And by the time it stopped outside the school gates, about three hundred and fifty grubby faces were poked through the school railings and seven hundred eyes were out on stalks.

It was a Jaguar. Twin carburettor. Sapphire blue. The tyres alone must have cost a hundred nicker apiece. My dad had told me. He had to be spot on with details like that in his line of work. When the door opened, the smell of leather and lifestyle shot up our noses (with a couple of capital Ls). When I was in my Millionaire Stockbroker phase this was exactly the sort of car I'd planned on having myself.

The new girl tossed us a glance as she stepped out – as if she were inspecting flea-ridden monkeys in a zoo. She was wearing a green uniform and a matching silly hat, gold braid plastered over both of them. It was obviously she'd been to a private school, and obvious she thought she was slumming it coming to a dump like ours.

She didn't smile as she stared at us. Her blonde hair was cut in a page boy style; her face was pale; her eyes were big and blue and expressionless. I could see straight away that she was what some people would call good-looking. But to me she looked cold and unreal – like those waxy flowers you see at funerals.

Her mother was out of the car now, and there was the same coldness about her, as if they'd both been carved from the same block of ice. She was wearing a dark blue two-piece costume with a white blouse, frilly bits at the neck. High heels. My mum would have called her smart.

She shut her door and locked it, then high-heeled it round to the zoo side of the car.

"Sure you have everything, darling?" she said in a voice that was too loud.

Darling didn't answer. I couldn't see her expression because she had her back to me.

But I could see Corvel's expression as he came out of the school gates to meet them. Lovely smile. First at the mother, then at the girl.

"Could I help you?" he said. "Would you

like to see the Headmaster?"

"That's awfully kind of you," said mummy iceberg.

"Let me show you the way," said Corvel.

We watched him escort them through the playground, chatting, friendly, smiling. What a terribly charming boy he really was!

And five minutes later the mother clicked her way back across the yard, looking even frostier and more up-tight than before.

The car door made a deliciously expensive chunky sound as she closed it. The engine purred, and the Jaguar slid and slid until it vanished round the corner in a puff of blue exhaust.

And five minutes later we were in assembly, hearing all about the poor little rich girl.

That was the second time in two days Mr Battrey took assembly. Which made me wonder if one of his microchips had gone on the blink.

The new girl stood just below him to his left. She didn't shuffle her feet or look up at the rafters, like any normal kid would. Just stared icily back at us like something whose grandmother had just sunk the *Titanic*.

"Good morning, school," Mr Battrey said, after Tarzan had barked out the usual changes in the timetable. You have to be Brain of Britain in our school, and that's just to catch the swimming bus. "Four things I'd like to talk to you about this morning, all of them important for the school's reputation. First the bad news, as they say. I'm afraid Miss Airey's waterproof compass has not yet been returned, and I have to report another lost dog. This one belongs to a Mrs Verny of 167 Omaney Road, and it went missing last week."

I didn't know Mrs Verny, but I knew Omaney Road all right. It was up Vista Hill from the traffic lights; genuine grotland. It used to have front gardens till they took them away to widen the link road to the motorway. Now there's just an iron barrier to stop you stepping out of your front door and under the wheels of an articulated lorry. Number 167 would be somewhere near the top.

"The missing dog is a liver and white spaniel that answers to the name of Charlie. If anybody has any information I should like to know."

That was it. He didn't go on about it like he had yesterday about Mrs Wright's dog. Maybe he was getting tired of dogs. Or maybe he just didn't like spaniels. Or maybe Mrs Verny, unlike Mrs Wright, had been married to a small shot, as opposed to a big one.

"Thirdly," Mr Battrey said, stiffening noticeably, "three tins of – ahum – food were – ahum – stolen from Mr Patel's – ahum – superstore last week. A girl in a blue dress was in his shop at the time. I do hope it wasn't –

ahum – someone from our school." He glanced down at Miss Frostbite as he spoke. "Which brings us to the good news. We have a new member of our school community to greet this morning. As some of you know, Lois was supposed to join us at the beginning of the term but for – ahum – reasons she has not been able to until now. Shall we welcome her in the usual way?"

As I clapped I wondered what ahum reasons had made Lois late.

"You know," said Mr Battrey as the clapping died down, "I was very proud of our school this morning as I looked out of my study window. Shall I tell you why? When Mrs DeWinter arrived, a boy from our school went up and immediately began to look after the new girl and her mother. That boy was Edwin Lawful – also new." (I told you names weren't his strong point, didn't I?) "Thank you, Edgar," he continued, nodding at Corvel. "That was very kind of you. You made me feel very proud as I sat there; I'm sure you made *all* of us feel very proud, and you can rest assured, Egbert, that your name shall not be forgotten."

Corvel lowered his head modestly and heaven sent an appropriate shaft of sunlight through a hole in the curtains to alight on his napper like a halo.

"You know, most of us are very lucky in our

little community, children. We know one another to start with. We don't have to say, 'Hello? Who are you?' I always think we're like one big happy family, don't you?"

Oh very, I thought. *Absolutely. One very big happy family, with Corvel at the centre of it, pinching everyone's Bubbly Bombs (not to mention their other things).*

"But have you ever thought what a new person coming to our school might feel like? They might feel strange for the first day or two. Everything will be different for them. They might even feel alone."

I wondered why Mr Battrey was making such a big deal of it.

"You know," he said, "coming into a community, a new person needs help. They need to know they're welcome. They need friends."

The new girl didn't look to me like she needed friends. Her eyes weren't saying *I need friends*. More: *Why don't you push off, frog-faces!*

"That's maybe especially important for Lois because – " He coughed and adjusted his specs. "Because," he went on, "she's arrived at an – ahum – awkward time."

I couldn't see anything ahum awkward about it. It was fish fingers for dinner, and – for our class – swimming in the afternoon. What could have been more appropriate than that?

"So I would like you to make Lois especially welcome. Mr McGeorge, if you would kindly take over..."

After we'd been dismissed, Charlotte and Lester caught me up in the corridor.

"Do you think he was right?" Charlotte asked me.

"About what?"

"About helping the new girl."

"Not by the look on her face," I said.

"People sometimes look like that when they're lonely," said Lester.

"Lester," I replied, "people look like that when they're snobs."

"I think we should take her, Rodney," said Charlotte.

"Where?" I said. "Siberia? I think she's already been."

"You know what Charlotte means," said Lester. "Take her in our gang."

"No way," I said.

"Aren't we going to do anything, Rodney?" asked Charlotte.

"Sure we are," I said. "Tonight we're going to see Mrs Verny."

TEN

Dad hadn't come down for tea that day – he often didn't at this stage in proceedings – and when Lester magnanimously volunteered to take Oscar out for his walkies Mum said, "Why don't you take Dad his mug of tea up, Rodney? You know he'd appreciate that."

"Do I have to, Mum?"

"You can't carry on like this, Rodney," she said, looking at me meaningfully as she put away the bread knife. "Not with your dad at this stage. You have to be reasonable. You're acting like a child."

"Mother, I *am* a child," I reminded her. "In any case," I said, "what about Dad? Why does it always have to be me that gives in?"

"It's not a case of giving in, Rodney. We know that at your age boys can feel awkward about their fathers, but this is just silly."

"I don't know what you're talking about, Mum!" I said. (But she was dead right, of course.)

"If you do go up, you could tell him I've put his fish pie back in the oven," she said. "And don't forget his sugar."

Dad was standing in the middle of his room

when I went up, wreathed in smoke and looking like a convincing argument for mercy killing at the age of forty. The carpet slippers he wore were so old that they would have had the experts on the *Antiques Roadshow* frothing with excitement.

As I stood there, holding the tray and trying my best to look the dutiful Number One son, I wondered if I was fated to be like that myself in thirty years' time; it seemed a fate worse than death.

He hardly saw me. He was staring mad-eyed at the Plan which he'd stuck to the wall. Every little street was marked on it: the name of every little pub and takeaway, every little aspect meticulously planned to the last detail, nothing left to chance. He always said that was why everything always went so smoothly.

"I've brought your tea, Dad," I said.

"Oh," he said. "Thanks, Rodney. Very kind of you."

I shoved aside a heap of papers on his desk so I could set down the tray, and in doing so uncovered a revolver. It was surprisingly heavy. I found it impossible to hold at arm's length without my hand wavering.

"Is it real, Dad?" I asked.

"Only a replica. I don't need the real thing, not for this job!"

"Of course," I said.

He looked at me and smiled, but his mind

was already drifting elsewhere. It always was at this stage. He lit his pipe and waggled the match to make it go out, but it didn't, not quite.

"You've set fire to your beard, Dad," I said after a moment, trying to sound calm.

"Have I? So I have! Thought I could smell singeing somewhere!"

He patted out the forest fire and dropped the match on the carpet where it made burn mark number 1000001.

"How's things, son?"

I knew he meant the Quibble saga, which Lester had blabbed about.

"Fine, Dad," I said.

He looked at me.

"Mum going out on another of her demos tonight?"

"Yep."

I agreed with him about Mum's demos. In my opinion, mums were made for steamed puddings and properly ironed shirts. In any case, it was all crazy. She and a few others had got it into their heads that for weeks the government had been transporting nuclear waste through the borough. As if the government would do anything like that!

"And how's school?" he asked, edging a fraction nearer Miss Quibble.

"OK. Fine."

"Good. I'm sorry we're going through a bad patch, Rodney. It's probably my fault."

"It's OK, Dad. It's probably mine."

"It's nobody's fault, son," he said. "It's the stages we're at. Both of us. Part of Life's Big Plan." Mention of which must have jogged his memory because his gaze slid back to that other Plan, the one on the wall, and his eyes started glassing over. He lit another match and set fire to his beard again.

I don't think he noticed me go out.

When I got downstairs, Charlotte had arrived. She was helping Mum sort out her demo stuff while they listened to the government minister on the telly assuring everybody that it was unthinkable that nuclear waste was being carried through London. Anybody could see with their eyes shut the man was honest. He had a square jaw, looked straight at the camera as he spoke and – to clinch matters – his eyes were almost further apart than his ears.

"How's your dad?" asked Mum.

"Fine," I said. "He's just set fire to his beard twice."

"Everything's normal, then. You told him about the fish pie?"

"I forgot about the fish pie," I said.

"Everything's normal!" said Charlotte.

"They're a pair!" Mum said to her.

Charlotte laughed, and Lester returned with Oscar.

"We really ought to take him with us

tonight, Rodney," he said. "He's got one heck of a nose."

"I've noticed," I said. "You mean for lamp-posts?"

"You should've seen him outside number eleven," said Lester. "I think maybe he's got some bloodhound in him."

I looked at Oscar. It was true that his eyes were droopy. But then, the rest of him drooped as well.

"Are you going somewhere special to-night?" asked Mum.

"A lady up Omaney Road has lost her dog," explained Charlotte, "and we're going to try and help her find it."

"That's very kind of you," said Mum.

"That's exactly why we should take Oscar," said Lester. "He might be able to track down her missing dog."

"It might not be a good idea to take a dog round to Mrs Verny's, Lester," said Charlotte. "It might upset her."

That's the trouble with my little brother. Unlike me, he's so insensitive.

ELEVEN

The clock of St Giles' church was striking half past six as we crossed the road at the bottom of Vista Hill. We had to wait ages before the lights changed – with lorries thundering past, trying to make up time after being slowed down on the motorway.

Hamilton was cruising around the cemetery gates on his skateboard. He waved at Lester, but gave me a nasty look.

"Why is Hamilton looking at you like that?" Lester asked. "He's a real nice kid."

"You could've fooled me!" I said.

"Desmond told me he's a real good boxer. He trains at some gym."

"A gym for what?" I asked. "Garden gnomes?"

Although Omaney Road is so near to where we live, it could have been another world. The houses had a tatty look to them, bits and pieces missing, as if they were surviving some kind of war; and the further you went up the hill, the worse the houses got.

Number 167 looked as if it had been attacked by machine-gun bullets. The house was divided into flats and there were six or seven door buzzers, each with a grubby piece of card stuck beside it. Hanging half off the wall was the speaker of some Stone Age intercom.

I pressed the appropriate buzzer.

After a minute we heard a voice say, "What you want?"

But not from the speaker. From behind us.

I turned round and discovered Hamilton with his skateboard tucked under his arm. He must have trailed all the way up the hill after us.

I didn't really want one of Corvel's spies hanging around.

"Why don't you take a ride on your skateboard, kid?" I asked him. "Preferably a long one."

He just stared at me. I remember thinking, *If there was ever a kid who wanted slapping down, it's this one!* Then he started up the hill.

"Press the buzzer again," said my brother.

"What for?" I said.

"I'd like to be home for Christmas."

I buzzed again. Nobody came. The church clock struck quarter to seven.

"I don't think she's in," said Charlotte.

I buzzed again.

Another pause.

The intercom clicked.

"Who is it?" said an old lady's voice over a sea of crackle.

An old lady who sounded scared to death.

* * *

In a typical flash of genius, I let Charlotte do the talking.

"Hello, Mrs Verny," she said through the speaker, "you don't know us, but this morning our headmaster told us about you losing your dog."

A pause.

"What about it?"

At that point I heard a noise behind me like the American Cavalry galloping to the rescue, and as I turned I saw the famous Hamilton had arrived back, this time with six of his diminutive friends, all balanced on their skateboards, like The Magnificent Seven Dwarfs on Wheels.

"You and your nasty pals better stop bugging the old lady," he said.

I must admit I was baffled by this remark. Nobody could have called Charlotte nasty. As for Lester. Thick. Obnoxious. Pain in the you-know-what. Yes, I admit all this, and worse. But not nasty. Not even Lester.

"Why don't you go and bury your head in the sand?" I asked him.

"We'd like to help you, Mrs Verny," Charlotte was saying.

"Who's with you?" Mrs Verny asked.

"Just two boys," said Charlotte. "We'd all like to help."

"Two boys?" said Mrs Verny. She didn't like the sound of that.

Hamilton obviously didn't approve of me,

either, but after a reassuring word from Lester he went up to the intercom and – by standing on tip-toe and straining his neck at the same time – was able to speak through it.

"It's OK, Mrs Verny," he said. "They're not the same boys who come round the other night."

"Who's that talking now?" she asked.

"Me, Mrs Verny. Hamilton."

"Hamilton who?"

"Hamilton DeFreitas. We just moved in. Remember?"

"Is that your real name?" I asked him.

"My real name's Hamilton the Third, if you want to know," he said, moving closer, the better to eyeball my kneecaps, "and we ain't scared of nobody, 'specially not you!"

He and his dwarfish confederates moved closer still: it was like being threatened by a handful of jelly babies.

"Has your dog come back yet, Mrs Verny?" asked Charlotte over the crackle.

(*We're so clever*, I was thinking, *we've split the atom, landed a man on the moon, but we still haven't mastered electric static!*)

Then, from Mrs Verny, "No, he hasn't."

"We'd like to help, only we can't help if you won't let us in."

Another crackle.

I really thought we were never going to get in to see her, but then we heard a door open inside the house, the shuffle of feet down the hall, and a moment later she'd opened the door. An old lady with her hair blowing in the wind and her stockings clustering round her ankles.

As we followed her down the passage there was a stink of tatie water and gas. I noticed a payphone, which I thought might come in handy. Rock music was blasting out through an open door on the next landing up and a full-sized version of Hamilton was leaning over the banisters. I couldn't read all of the message on his T-shirt because his brawny arms were crossed, but the top line said I MAKE and I could make out one letter of the third word – a U – so I guessed it was TROUBLE. *I bet!* I thought.

"What you kids up to?" he asked as we passed beneath him.

"Helping Mrs Verny," said Charlotte.

"Oh yeah?"

"Take no notice of him," said Mrs Verny when she'd shut the door behind us. "The police keep coming for him in a car and taking him away. I expect he's been up to something."

You could still hear the music, only now it seemed to be coming through the ceiling.

"Do you want Rodney to ask them to turn the noise down?" asked Charlotte.

"I don't want no trouble," said Mrs Verny, which I thought was just as well.

We were in a back room of the house, in

what had probably been the original kitchen, but was now where Mrs Verny lived her life. There was a single bed in the corner, an army of photos on the mantelpiece, a sink of dirty dishes, and something – a giant rat? – scratching at the door of a wall cupboard, waiting to bounce into the room.

"What's that noise, Mrs Verny?" asked Charlotte.

"Nothing," she said. "I can't hear nothing."

The next second the cupboard door popped open – I nearly died of fright – and a long-legged kitten, obviously in desperate need of relief, shot to the back door.

"Should I let your kitten out, Mrs Verny?" asked Charlotte.

"No," she said. She looked scared.

Charlotte tried to pick it up but it spat at her.

"She doesn't take to people," explained Mrs Verny.

"I think it might want to do something," said Charlotte.

"No," Mrs Verny insisted. "I never let her out at night. She has a tray over there if she wants to do something."

"What's its name?" asked Charlotte.

"Tiddles," said Mrs Verny.

Tiddles by name, and tiddles by nature, I thought as it hopped into the tray and went swiftly about its business.

"Are you friends of those other boys that

came to see me?" Mrs Verny asked when the excitement was over.

"What other boys?" I asked.

"Shall I clear this table and wash up, Mrs Verny?" asked Charlotte.

"Don't bother, dear. I'll do it when you're gone."

"It's no bother," said Charlotte, turning on a tap. "It won't take a minute. Which is your hot tap, Mrs Verny? This water's cold."

"I haven't the heating on yet, dear. I don't turn it on till later," she said, sitting at the table. "You'll have to use the kettle."

"Have these other boys come round tonight, Mrs Verny?" I asked.

"No," she said. "They haven't been tonight."

"When *did* they come?"

"I forget. Last week, I think. I get muddled with the dates."

"What were they like?" I asked.

"I forget now. I don't want to get them into trouble."

"Had one of them got fair hair?" I said.

"I couldn't say. I'd lost my specs at the time."

"I thought we might just know them at school," I said.

"I don't think you will. They come from another one."

"Which one?"

"I forget now. They was big boys."

"Was one of them smart?" I asked.

"No, scruffy. They was both scruffy. But very helpful. They said they wanted to help."

"Help?" I said. "How? You hadn't lost your dog then, had you?"

"I forget exactly how," she said, "but they was very nice." She glanced at the clock which said twenty past six. "I can't sit here and talk to you all night. My son'll be round any minute. He always comes at half past six, on the dot."

"Does he live near you, Mrs Verny?" asked Charlotte.

"Inkerman Road," she said. "It's just round the corner."

"That's nice. Where's your drying-up cloth, Mrs Verny?"

"Just leave them to drain, dear. I'll get one out when I remember. My son's one of them karate experts," she said, looking back at me.

"That's handy," I said, thinking of Corvel. I'd once started karate myself – during my Rambo phase – but I'd dropped out after one lesson: most of the other kids enjoyed colliding with walls and I just didn't think it was my scene. "I wonder why those boys came?" I asked her.

"I'm sure they wouldn't do nothing like that," said Mrs Verny.

"Like what, Mrs Verny?"

"Like what happened to Charlie. He was always a good dog. He never dashed across roads. I used to let him out every night. That's his red blanket," she said indicating one by the back door. "He always slept on that. It's ready there waiting for him when he comes back, I told the boys. He was always very sensible."

"But why did they come in the first place?" I said.

"You're getting me all confused," said Mrs Verny. "I don't like getting confused. My son'll be round any minute. He always comes about this time. He thinks the world of me, my son. That's a letter from him," she said, nodding at a letter on the mantelpiece with scrawly purple writing on it. "He gets that annoyed if anythink upsets me."

Quick as a flash I said, "But, Mrs Verny, why does he write to you if he lives just round the corner?"

Poor Mrs Verny looked blank for a moment.

"Maybe he used to work away, did he, Mrs Verny?" said Charlotte.

"That's right. He used to work away."

"On the oil-rigs, was it?" said Lester helpfully.

"That's right. On the oil-rigs."

My brother wandered over to the mantelpiece and stuck his big nose into her photos. I told you he had no idea.

"I do hope Charlie's all right," said Mrs

Verny. "He always used to look before he crossed the road, otherwise I would never have let him out. I never worried. Then last – Wednesday, was it? – I let him out and he never come back. He might still be all right, though."

"I'm sure he will be," said Charlotte, again trying unsuccessfully to pick up the kitten. "I'm sure he'll come back."

"I leave something out the back for him every night, just a bite to eat and a drink, and I leave the back yard gate open for him."

"It couldn't be the people upstairs who've taken him?" I said.

"They wouldn't do anything like that. They're just ignorant."

"I'll empty your rubbish for you, shall I?" my brother said.

"Don't bother," said Mrs Verny, but she was already too late and he'd gone out into the back yard and shut the door behind him.

"Has anybody else suspicious called on you in the last few days, Mrs Verny?" I asked. "No tramps, for instance, with big black beards?"

"No. Only my son. Like I say, he comes round every night."

"No Girl Guides?"

"Oh no," she said. "No Girl Guide has ever set foot in this house."

My brother came back in and put the rubbish bin under the sink again.

"There we are, Mrs Verny," he said. "All

nice and tidy."

"That's very kind of you," said Mrs Verny, "but I'll have to ask you to go now. My son does get in a nasty temper when he does come."

"Does he?" I said, smiling. "In that case, Mrs Verny, we'd better go. We don't want to be karate-chopped to death, do we? You've been very helpful, and we'll see what we can do."

TWELVE

"Well, that definitely proves it!" I said as we hit the pavement.

"Proves what, Rodney?" asked Charlotte. "That Corvel stole this dog as well, you mean?"

"Who else are the two boys she's scared of?"

As we started down the hill I kept a sharp look out for Hamilton, in case I tripped over him and his skateboard, but for the moment he seemed to have vanished. Looking further ahead, however, the news was not so cheery: the usual crowd of protesters – no doubt including my mother – had gathered outside St Giles' and were waving their pathetic banners.

"She did say the boys were both big, Rodney," said Charlotte. "And Corvel's smaller than you."

"She also said she'd lost her specs, Charlotte," I reminded her.

"If she'd lost her specs, Hercules Porridge," said my little brother, "that would have made them smaller, not bigger, wouldn't it?"

"Stop trying to score points, Lester," I said. "The point is, Mrs Verny was scared."

"That is true, Rodney," said Charlotte. "On the other hand, she did say they were scruffy."

"She probably said that about them being big and scruffy to throw us off the scent," I said.

"But why should she want to do that?" asked Charlotte.

"Because she's scared. You know what Corvel is like."

"Just because *you*'re scared of Corvel it doesn't mean everybody is," said my little brother.

"*I*'m not scared of him!" I said.

"Not much!" said Lester. "You always have been."

"I haven't! Come to that, *everybody*'s scared of Corvel."

"I'm not!" said my little brother.

"Oh, no?"

"Let's not get into stupid arguments again," said Charlotte.

"Quite right, Charlotte," I said. "We are being diverted from the real point because of unnecessary interruptions."

"You mean you should talk and everybody else should listen?" said Lester.

"The point is," I said, ignoring him, "the old lady was scared to death when she first came to the door. She didn't even want to open it. Especially when she heard there were two boys. Why? Because she most probably thought we were Corvel and Byrne. Point Number Two: why do you think she never lets the kitten out? Because she's scared that it'll go the same way as the dog. That's what Corvel is up to: he's nicking people's dogs. That's why she's scared of him. That's why she said he was from a different school: because she doesn't want all this to get back to him. And how does she know he's from a different school when none of us had our uniforms on?"

"But we don't even know it *was* Corvel," said Lester. "She didn't seem too keen on the folks upstairs, either. Does that mean *they* stole the dog as well?"

"Why do you have to go around making yourself look ridiculous, little brother?" I said. "Just because people play loud rock music, that doesn't mean they're the sort who go about nicking dogs."

"The music could be to cover up the sound of the barking," he said.

"Point Number Three," I said, speaking mainly to Charlotte. "Did anybody notice Mrs Verny's face when I mentioned the Girl Guide?"

"She definitely did look guilty," said Charlotte. "I agree with you there, Rodney."

"She was lying through her false teeth," I said. "All that codswallop about Girl Guides never setting foot in her house was lies. And, of course, it all links up with the Guide who was at Mrs Wright's."

"Pardon me for asking," said my brother, "but are you now trying to suggest that Corvel came once as himself with Byrne, and then disguised as the Girl Guide?"

"It's possible," I said. "You never saw him in the nativity play, Lester. You were hardly born in those days."

"I felt sorry for her," said Charlotte. "She was lonely."

"Charlotte," I said, "it's no good letting our emotions get entangled with these things. We're here to solve a crime."

"That *is* a sort of crime, isn't it?" said Charlotte.

"What do you mean?"

"That people have to live like that."

"It's probably their own fault," I said. "People have to learn to help themselves."

"But how can she, Rodney? That's just stupid."

"It isn't. It's sensible. Besides, she has her son. And he's just the sort of son she needs to deal with Corvel and Byrne. He's probably round there by now. What I'd like to see is Byrne and Corvel call on her again and walk straight into him."

"You noticed her clock, Sherlock Bones?" asked my little brother. "It said twenty past six when she said her son was due."

"So?"

"It's only that the church clock was striking half past as we passed it on our way there. That means Mrs Verney's clock was near

75

enough three-quarters of an hour slow. In other words, her son should have been there before we were."

As if to prove his point, the clock of St Giles' struck half past seven as we passed the church front. Glancing in that direction, I happened to see my mother in the thick of the rent-a-mob. Mothers can be terribly embarrassing at times. I turned away and pressed the button-thing to change the lights.

"She was probably making allowances for the clock," I said.

"That's possible. There's only one snag," said my brother.

"What's that?"

"I don't think Mrs Verny's telling the truth about her son."

"What you on about now?" I said.

"I began to suspect that when I had a close look at the letter he was supposed to have written."

"I noticed you shoving your nose in!"

"If she has a son, he's called Ada."

"What do you mean?"

"That's how the letter was signed."

"Are you sure?"

"I *can* read three-letter words, Rodney. I also looked at all her photos on the mantelshelf. There was no picture of any son."

"Wowee!" said Charlotte who – like all girls – is easily impressed.

"There *was* a picture of Charlie," my little brother went on. "Liver and white spaniel, just like the Head said. And a picture of Tiddles. *And* what was probably her husband, in his army uniform – and a couple of old fogeys who were probably her mum and dad. But no picture of a son of any shape or form. One other thing…" – he just loves showing off – "You know when I went outside to empty the rubbish? The back yard gate was locked, with a bolt. And there was no dog food out there."

"You sure about that, Lester?" said Charlotte.

"Positive."

"Maybe the next door's cat ate it," I said.

"Good thinking, Sherlock," said my little brother, "but there's only one little snaglet. There was no bowl either. Though of course the cat could have eaten the bowl as well!"

I didn't say anything. I wondered if I'd made a wrong move opting for the detective business. I wondered if I should plunge straight into some other, more suitable phase. Like diving over cliffs without a parachute, for instance. Maybe it was time I washed my hands of the whole thing.

I felt devastated, flattened, and finished. I couldn't stand any more of my clever little brother, so after we'd crossed the road I dropped back and pretended my trainers needed fastening.

And it was a lucky thing I did.

Because as I passed number eleven, I suddenly saw the light.

Or, rather, I saw the tramp going round the back of number eleven – not a light in the place – carrying a plastic bag from which came the merry clink of empty bottles. My little brother didn't notice because he was walking ahead, jawing on about his own cleverness. But the moment I saw the tramp, the scales dropped from my teeth, as they say, and I realized that all this time I'd been barking up the wrong horse.

You get it? The tramp we'd seen calling at Mrs Wright's was squatting in number eleven. Which explained everything. For instance:

1. It *had* been the tramp I'd seen in the basement of number eleven.

2. It explained why Mrs Wright's side gate had been bolted when the dog had flown. It wasn't Corvel who'd taken the dog after all: it was the tramp. He'd hopped over the low fence at the bottom of her garden, same as we had.

3. The tramp fitted in nicely with Mrs Verny's description: big and scruffy. In fact he was almost too big for any school but, as we know, she was without her specs at the time, and that – if experts are to be believed – would make him appear smaller.

4. It suggested the possible whereabouts of *both* dogs.

5. It probably tied in with the shoplifting from Mr Patel's superstore as well. Remember what Mr Battrey had said? *Three tins of ahum food were ahum stolen*. Well now I had a pretty good idea of what kind of food it was.

The only question still puzzling me was: *If it wasn't Corvel who'd overheard us in our garden shed, who was it?* It could hardly have been the tramp: he wouldn't have had time to get back down into number eleven's basement. And even if he had, he would hardly draw attention to himself by lighting a candle and calling out. So who was it?

All the same, I felt quietly chuffed as I rejoined Charlotte and Lester. I was now pretty certain who had taken the dogs and – most probably – the tins of ahum food as well, though naturally I didn't breathe a word of this at the time. I only had to mention the tramp to Lester, and he would imagine that he'd been the first to suspect him, and try to claim all the glory for himself. He was that kind of kid.

Tomorrow, without telling anyone, I would go to Mr Battrey and make certain about that ahum food.

THIRTEEN

Next morning as I crossed the yard, I saw Mr Battrey sitting at his desk and it occurred to me he had been plugged in there all night.

In his outer office his fellow computers were already churning out memoranda, keeping up a *bleep-bleep* among themselves as they worked, like a herd of electronic sheep. Of Mr Battrey's secretary, the divine Miss Byeline, there was unhappily neither sight nor sound.

Glancing at the line of buttons at the side of Mr Battrey's door, I saw the one marked ENGAGED: PLEASE RING was lit up. I rang it, idly wondering as I did so if the button not only alerted the Head but actually switched him on as well. Did little lights pop on inside him, I wondered, as if in a pinball machine?

Almost at once Miss Byeline shot out, closing the door behind her.

"What is it you want, Rodney?" she asked.

She looked flushed and discomposed, and I guessed that the Mean Machine beyond the door had been upsetting her.

"If it's humanly possible," I said, "I'd like to speak to Mr Battrey."

My punny remark seemed to pass her by.

"He's chairing the Inter-Curricular Sub-

Committee for Provisional Planning in ten minutes," she said.

"Wow!" I said. "That sounds mega-important!"

"It is, Rodney. So don't be all day – you know what you're like. Five minutes and no longer!"

"Ah!" said Mr Battrey, glancing up from behind three VDU screens clustered before him. His face, bathed in green, looked decidedly fishy. "Nice to see you again, Richard."

"Rodney, sir," I said.

"Pencilcase, isn't it?"

"Penfold, sir."

"Right you are!" he said, as if confirming my opinion. He punched a key. "Got you now. Penfold, Rodney. 3Pi. Favourite colour: Blue. Ambition: To become a writer."

"That was last week, sir," I said.

"Changed our mind have we?"

"That's right, sir."

"Be so good as to inform Miss Byeline when you go out, will you, Rodney? We do like to keep these things up to date. Now, looking again, our data tells me your hobbies are collecting poisonous snakes, savage scorpions, and conkers. Is that still substantially correct?"

"Exactly right, sir."

I'd only put that in about poisonous snakes and scorpions to practise my alliteration, and the conkers bit had been true aeons ago – last term, to be exact – but I'd forgotten to cross it out on the card.

"Computers never make mistakes," said Mr Battrey. "Never forget that."

"I won't, sir."

"And it's all in there, Pinfold. Every little bit about every single child in the school."

"Isn't that dangerous, sir?"

"Confidentiality, you mean? Not at all. The really confidential material is on the red terminal out there." He nodded his head to indicate the outer office. "And you'd have to be jolly clever to get at it – almost as clever as I am!" He laughed at the sheer impossibility of such a thing. "Now how can I help you, Roger?"

"It's about the dogs, sir."

"Dogs?" He turned round and looked anxiously out of his window into the yard. "Don't tell me we've been invaded by animal life again?"

"The dogs you mentioned in assembly, sir. Don't you remember?"

"I never remember anything, Ronald," he said, not without a hint of triumph. He pressed a couple more keys. "Why should I, when it's all on floppy disc? Computers are marvellous tools, Ralph, though there are certain functions which they cannot perform and it is these other, higher, functions which we humans must concentrate on."

"You mean like blowing our noses, sir?"

"Not exactly. Here we are. You're quite right, I *did* mention dogs in assembly. Now how can I help you?"

"It's just that I think I know what's happened to the dogs, sir. Somebody's stolen them."

"Really?" He leaned forward to whisper, "Nobody in school I hope?"

"No, sir."

"Thank heavens for that!" he said. "That wouldn't be at all good for our image. Might we enquire whom you suspect?"

"A tramp, sir."

"A tramp, eh? That sounds ideal. Likely, too. Reminds me of a story I once read. I'm so relieved. SCHOOL GIRL STEALS DOGS wouldn't be a nice headline to see in the local paper."

"No, sir."

"You're sure this tramp has no connection with the school? He's not by any chance an old boy or anything like that?"

"I don't think so, sir. He's definitely scruffy."

"Jolly good. Splendid. Well, keep up the good work, Rudolph, and now if you'll excuse me, I have to take the chair at a meeting."

"That one, sir?" I asked, pointing at the one he was sitting in.

He looked round at the chair, and then at me – blankly.

"That was a joke, sir," I explained.

"A joke?" He seemed to be confused and I wondered if the word hadn't been included in his program. "Oh! I see! Well done, Roy! Very droll. Jolly good. Ha! Ha! It was very kind of you to come. Is that all?"

"You also mentioned in assembly some shoplifting from Mr Patel's superstore, sir. I'd like to ask a question about that."

"Ahum," he said.

"What's the matter, sir?"

"Nothing – ahum – at all. Why do you want to know about the shoplifting?"

"It's just that I think the two things may be connected, sir."

"Impossible, Rupert. They can't – ahum – be."

"Why not, sir?"

"The computer doesn't think so. And – ahum – computers never lie."

"But I think the tramp might be involved in them both, sir."

"Ah!" he said, "that's different! You may very well be right there, Raphael." He pressed a key. "Here we are. Assembly, Tuesday. All the information you require, Robert. Shoplifting. Three tins of – ahum – food. How's that for efficiency?"

"Fine, sir. What kind of ahum food was it?"

"Just a tick. Have to punch up a sub-file." He punched three keys. "Kind of – ahum – food: animal."

"What kind of ahum animal was it, sir?"

"Just a tick." Punch. Punch. His face flickered greenly.

"Got it," he said. "You can always rely on computers, Rory. Cat."

"Cat?"

"Cat."

"You're sure it was cat, sir? Not dog?"

"Cat," he said. "Computers never lie. Did I mention that before?"

I decided to be charitable and said, "I'm not sure, sir. I can't always remember."

"Do try to develop your memory, my boy," he said. "Always remember, it's your finest tool, Raymond."

"I will, sir," I said, beating a retreat.

FOURTEEN

I worked flat out all through R.E. Not at R.E. of course. Nobody ever worked in Mrs Postle's lessons. Everybody either messed about or did their maths homework.

No, I worked hard at what in my mind I was already calling The Case of the Disappearing Dogs.

I was delighted that Mr Battrey also thought the tramp a prime suspect, but it was a definite setback that the tins stolen had contained cat food instead of dog food. I couldn't wangle my way round that problem, not just yet. And it also worried me that at first Mr Battrey had been so keen to separate the shoplifting from the disappearing dogs. Why was that?

Altogether everything was beginning to look as clear as primeval mud, and I must have looked slightly confused and disappointed when I reported to Charlotte and Lester in the yard at breaktime.

"So I'm feeling a bit cheesed off," I admitted when I'd finished.

"Hard Cheddar!" said my punny little brother.

Charlotte smiled at me encouragingly.

If you're the kind of person I am – imaginative, sensitive, and modest – you need encouragement, and I almost smiled back, but couldn't quite make it. If I'd been Sherlock Bones at that moment, I'd have been puffing exasperated puffs from my meerschaum pipe, or throwing all thirty volumes of the *Universal Medical Dictionary* at Dr Witless's head.

"You still feel the shoplifting and the dogs are connected?" said Charlotte.

I nodded at her.

"It could be they're the sort of dogs that prefer cat food," said my little brother.

"That's not funny, Lester," said Charlotte.

"Who's trying to be funny?" he said. "I'm trying to be helpful. Look at it another way: is the cat food really a red herring?"

"What makes you think the two dogs are connected, Rodney?" Charlotte asked me.

"It's always possible they fell in love and eloped together," said Lester.

At that moment Tarzan crashed through the door – he always crashed through it like a bull entering the arena – and stood there steaming in his tracksuit. He was obviously looking for some kind of trouble to sort out. Unfortunately, of Corvel there was no sign. There never was when the duty teacher was around. He was probably in the bogs, shaking Mintos out of some poor kid.

The most conspicuous thing in the yard was the new girl. And Tarzan was staring at her, hard, with the gormless animal look in his eye that always came so naturally to him.

It was easy to see what was going through his simple mind: *I'm going to get you, girl!* But I couldn't think why at the time.

Not that I had much sympathy for her, mind you. She was still wearing her snobby uniform and was standing all alone at the top end of the yard, her back against the wall. It's a good place to stand when the cold wind doth blow and we shall have snow, but today was a mild September day. Wet chestnut leaves were plastered all over the playground like soggy ducks' feet. So there was no excuse.

She was standing all alone because she didn't want any friends. She was that sort. She enjoyed sticking out like a sore toe. She reminded me of an old film star my mother was keen on, a real old crumbly whose first name was Greta and second name something like Cardboard. She, too, had a pageboy haircut and eyes that were blue and sad. My dad always said she looked like that because she'd just lost her hamburger. "*I vont to be alone,*" she kept saying. Vich vos probably vy she vos alvays surrounded by menk. And the new girl was like that. She, too, probably vonted to be alone.

Well, she'd got what she wanted.

And she was certainly the centre of attention, at least as far as Tarzan was concerned.

"Why is he looking at her like that?" asked Charlotte.

"Ask me another," I said.

"Why do you hate her so much, Rodney?" Charlotte said.

"I don't. That's just ridiculous."

"At least the Jag didn't bring her this morning," said Lester.

Yes, it was true. The new girl had actually walked to school this morning, on her own two feet. Her rich mummy hadn't brought her. Big deal!

The bell went for the end of break.

Tarzan's knees started twitching. He breathed fire and barked out his orders and we all started moving towards the entrance like obedient bunny-wabbits. All except the new girl. She hesitated just a moment before she pushed herself off the wall, as if showing unwilling.

Tarzan noticed that. He glared at her. He almost swung through the litter and finished her off with a savage bite of his fangs.

"I do wish we could help her, Rodney," Charlotte said.

"I agree," said Lester. "Why don't we?"

"I've told you both," I said. "That type doesn't need friends."

It was what I honestly believed at the time.

FIFTEEN

All through maths I pondered deeply on pet food, though it isn't as easy to fool Mr Rangle as it is Mrs Postle. In maths you have to *appear* to be working even if you're not, because if you're not swallowing your tongue and screwing your eyeballs into your head, Mr Rangle isn't totally happy – and if he isn't totally happy he has a tendency to fly down your aisle dishing out sarky remarks like, "Left our so-called brains at home this morning, have we, Penfold?" Or else he accidentally-on-purpose whops you one over the napper with his answer book.

So I was pleased with myself when I came out into the yard at dinner time with my head still more or less where it was supposed to be, yet having thought my way neatly round the Great Cat Food Problem. It was obvious, really. The tramp was rounding up dogs *and* cats. It all linked up beautifully with Mrs Verny keeping Tiddles in the cupboard.

"You seriously believe that?" asked my little brother. "Then how come we haven't heard of any missing mogs?"

"Because people don't value cats so much. Don't you know anything?"

"That's not true, Rodney," said Charlotte.

"As a matter of fact I mentioned this cat food problem to Desmond last period," said Lester (*Desmond flipping Fiely again!* I thought), "and he reckons people feed their dogs on cat food because there's more protein in it. He reckons some old pensioner's been living on it for donkey's years."

"That's awful!" said Charlotte.

"It probably isn't even true, Charlotte," I said. "Where does he get these ridiculous ideas from, anyhow?"

"It was on the BBC news last night," said Desmond, who had crept up behind me.

I was just about to tell him where to stuff his nutty idea when I noticed that all round me kids were shifting like a herd of twitchy gazelles. At first I wondered if – for once – Tarzan had swung silently into the yard, then realized this was a contradiction in terms. Looking round, I saw there was no sign of him.

But I *could* see somebody else.

I don't think I've mentioned how silent Corvel could be. Silence is supposed to be one of the old-fashioned virtues, isn't it? *Silence is golden* is one of my mother's sayings: she usually trots it out when I am offering her advice. If it is a virtue, it must be the only one Corvel has.

Not that it makes him any better. What I

mean is, Corvel doesn't have to speak to make your flesh creep. He just has to look at you. And when he smiles you know you're in worse trouble. When he's in one of his smiley moods, kids (particularly in the younger classes) congregate in droves and slip through the gaps in the school railings to vanish into the park for the rest of the day.

And Corvel was smiling now.

Everybody in the yard knew it. Corvel doesn't have to break doors off their hinges to claim your attention. He just has it to start with.

He waited until nobody was moving. Then he started across the yard, still smiling.

My legs turned to diluted water when I saw that smile. But as he walked straight past me I thought, *Praise be to God!* because I realized it wasn't me he was after.

He was heading towards the new girl, still in the same place she'd been that morning, back against the wall. And when he reached her, he leaned forward and whispered something to her.

There was no reaction from the new girl. I could see her clearly.

He spoke again, moving nearer.

That was when I noticed something about Corvel and the new girl, she staring at him, her eyes blue and bored, like the actress who'd mislaid the hamburger. Something I hadn't noticed before. Something *really* important to my processes of deduction. *Sheer genius!* I thought.

Corvel moved a step nearer.

To be honest I still didn't feel sorry for the girl at that moment. I felt she was just getting what she deserved for being so snobby.

Corvel leaned forward and again whispered in her ear.

That was when she hit him.

There was no warning. Not a flicker of change in the icicle eyes. I think she must have hit him in the chest, hard. We all heard the thump.

I seemed to feel it myself. (Did I mention how sensitive I was?)

Corvel staggered and fell on his backside.

Nobody laughed. If anybody else had been pushed on their backside it would have been a hoot. But nobody laughed at Corvel. To be honest, when Corvel fell on his bottom, it wasn't funny at all. It was tragic.

We all knew what would be going through his horrible mind. And at that moment I *did* feel sorry for the new girl. If I'd been her at that moment, I'd have been praying. Hard.

But *she* wasn't praying.

The same cold look was in her eyes. She was looking down at Corvel almost as if he weren't there. As if he didn't exist.

He got up.

I don't think there was a single, solitary sound in that playground.

He went towards her again, faster, urgently. I'd never seen Corvel like that before. There were white blotches on his face. His hands were stretched forward. I don't know what he intended. It looked like he was about to grab her neck.

But he never managed it.

I'm not quite sure what happened. There was a sharp explosion of breath. Her fist shot out again, only harder this time, and Corvel went down again on his backside, and this time he didn't get up.

Byrne moved towards her, but stopped all of a sudden when he saw the look in her eyes. Anybody would have done: she'd adopted a strange kind of pose. Like a praying mantis.

For a moment everything was still.

Then she took two steps towards Corvel, leaned over him, and whispered something in *his* ear.

You could have knocked me down with a feather. I think the whole universe must have stood still at that moment. I wouldn't have been surprised to learn that the Head had given his computers a holiday.

Then the school door crashed against the wall as Tarzan bounced into the yard.

"What's going on here?" he shouted, his

quick brain telling him something was amiss.

Everything went back to normal again, if that's what it's called. Kids began whirligigging about the yard, screams began to be screamed. Corvel had picked himself up now and was bending over as he dusted down his trousers.

"What's the matter with you, Corvel?" Tarzan asked. "There's no need to bow down to me, you know!" He laughed. Everybody laughed because they knew if they didn't he might force them to smell his honky socks. "Don't forget it's the soccer practice tonight, Byrne," he said.

"I won't, sir," said Byrne.

He'd make an excellent footballer, Byrne. He'd really enjoy knocking people down and then walking all over their necks in his studded boots.

Tarzan glanced up at the new girl again. The same hard glance.

She was back against the wall now, as if she'd never moved. She looked calm, rather pleased in a quiet sort of way, as if she'd managed to locate the hamburger after all.

"That new girl," I said to Charlotte. "You can ask her if she'd like to join us, when we go in for dinner, if you want to. Tell her about the dogs. Tell her it's Corvel we suspect. And, Charlotte," I added, "I bet you anything, you like she doesn't want to know!"

"How d'you work that out, Rodney?" she asked me.

"All will be revealed in Chapter Thirty-one," I told her enigmatically.

SIXTEEN

I was just going into second sitting when Miss Quibble grabbed me again about the stupid detective story.

"I still don't think it's me, miss," I said.

"Nonsense, Rodney. Could I possibly see you at the end of school? I do want to get this thing moving. Four o'clock all right?"

"OK, miss," I said.

By the time I got to the dining-hall, most of the tables were full. I was glad to see Charlotte was already engaging El Frozen One in deep converse. Their table was otherwise empty and I could guess why: kids wouldn't want to associate themselves with somebody who had earned Corvel's displeasure (not if they wanted to live, that is).

I could have sat there, of course. Personally, I wasn't scared of Corvel. It was just that some things are best left to women. Not the really important stuff, of course. But they do have their uses.

The only other table with a space was occupied by my little brother, Hamilton the Third and Desmond Fiely. So I had no option.

"By the way," Lester said as I clattered my eating irons on the table, "Desmond thinks your Corvel-disguised-as-Girl-Guide idea really stinks."

"You amaze me," I said.

Of course, since noticing the startling similarity between Corvel and the new girl, I had kissed goodbye to the idea of Corvel's involvement, but I wasn't going to tell that to a twit like Desmond Fiely.

"Desmond says it's like – what's that big word again, Desmond?"

"It's like trying to make the facts fit your preconceived ideas," said Desmond, looking at me like a constipated owl. "Like Procrustes."

"Who's Pie Crusties when he's all there?" I asked.

"I told you he wouldn't know!" giggled Lester.

"Procrustes was this giant in ancient Greek legend," announced Wise Old Owl. "He used to invite travellers to sleep the night in his cave and if they didn't fit his bed he either cut bits off them or stretched them till they did fit."

"This doesn't sound to me like the sort of thing Girl Guides do, Desmond," I said. "Do they get a badge for it?"

"He still doesn't understand," Lester said. "Tell him about the acting, Desmond – he won't understand about that either!"

I stabbed my sausage, thinking how much I would have preferred to stab Lester or dozy Desmond, but Life is full of compromises round where we live.

"Yeah! Yeah!" said Hamilton. "Sock it to him, Dezzy!"

"Put it this way, Rodney," said Desmond. "It's really hard for a boy to pass himself off as a girl, especially to a woman. Remember Huckleberry Finn?"

"Whose class is he in?" I asked him.

"He's in a book by Mark Twain, Rodney. In one scene Huck dresses up as a girl but this woman knows he's a boy straight off because she chucks a lump of lead at him and he claps his knees together even though he's got a dress on."

"Mrs Wright isn't the sort who chucks lumps of lead about," I said.

"I *knew* he wouldn't get it!" said Lester.

I stabbed another sausage.

"Besides," I said, "Corvel is a good actor. Maybe you never saw him as the angel Gabriel in our school nativity play, Desmond."

"He's obsssessed about that!" said Lester.

"In any case," I said, "Corvel *looks* like a girl to start with."

"Oh, yeah?" said my little brother. "Why don't you tell him that?"

I looked up and saw that Corvel had just come into the hall. He didn't have school dinners; he always had sandwiches. Other people's sandwiches. He was standing just inside the door, helping himself to the Squit's crisps – while the dinner supervisor was yacking to Miss Byeline. The Squit was looking across at our table, as if for help: for some reason he seemed to be looking at me.

"Somebody ought to deal with that guy!" said Desmond.

"Quite right, Desmond," I said. "Why don't you start now?"

Before going out, Corvel looked across at the new girl and gave her one of his smiles. Then he glanced at the Squit, who went out with his lunchbox though he obviously hadn't finished. Presumably Corvel was feeling peckish.

"One day I'll fix him!" said Desmond, speaking as if through clenched teeth (but it may just have been a pea stuck in his mouth).

"Cool it, man, Dezzy, what can you do?" said Hamilton. Which was quite right. Desmond couldn't have floored a limping leprechaun. But then Hamilton said, "One of these days *I*'ll fix him!" which was ridiculous because if Hamilton had thrown a straight left he would have connected with Corvel's kneecap and wouldn't even have dented it.

At that moment Mr Battrey came in. For some reason he looked at the new girl for quite a time. He seemed worried. Then he glanced round and happened to see Miss Byeline, and his face changed dramatically. He went quite red. Poor Miss Byeline was so upset she went red, too. She said something quickly to the dinner supervisor and went out – I guessed he didn't like her taking a break, even at dinner time. He probably regarded her as some kind of machine.

"There's only one way to settle Corvel's hash," Desmond was muttering, "if that's what we really want to do."

"What's that?" I asked.

He didn't answer. Just stared at me like young Einstein in granny specs. As a matter of fact they were all three looking at me. As if I should know what they were talking about.

"You're the only one who's done karate, Rodney," said my little brother.

It was typical of him to kick me when I was down.

"What do you mean?" I said. "I only went once. All I learnt was how to breathe in properly and fall on a mat without breaking my neck in three places. Why are you looking like that? You guys must be crazy!"

But they continued to stare at me like a line of hungry puppies waiting to be fed.

It was lucky for me that the new girl stood up and went out at that moment, leaving Charlotte all alone, which gave me an excuse to move.

"Excuse me, gentlemen," I said. "Business calls."

I wandered over to her.

Lois had turned her down flat. Just as I had guessed she would.

"What did you tell her?" I asked Charlotte.

"More or less everything. The funny thing is, she seemed interested at first – till I told her we suspected Corvel."

"Then what did she say?"

"Just said she didn't want to get involved," said Charlotte.

I could see by her face she was disappointed.

"I told you," I said.

"I think she's too proud," said Charlotte.

"It isn't that," I said.

"What is it, then, Rodney? I still feel she needs help."

"It's facts we have to look at, Charlotte," I said kindly. "Not feelings."

"Facts *are* feelings, Rodney," said Charlotte. "Sometimes." She looked up at me. "I'd just like one more go at her."

"Sure," I said. "Why not? One thing, though. This time tell her it *isn't* Corvel we suspect."

"Isn't it? Who is it, then, Rodney? The tramp?"

"No. It's neither of them. Just tell her we suspect somebody else."

"Who, though, Rodney?"

"Just leave it vague, Charlotte," I said. "And I bet you anything she joins us like a shot."

SEVENTEEN

"Not even if I offered you *two* mints, Rodney?" said Miss Quibble.

"I'm not particularly fond of mints, miss," I said. I could still see Oscar's teeth marks.

"You'd be perfect for the job, Rodney," she said.

"I wouldn't, miss."

"Why are you being so coy?"

"What's coy mean, miss?"

"Playing hard to get." She shoved a load of exercise books in her shoulder-sack. She had to mark all that tonight. It wouldn't have been so bad if it was the sort of stuff I wrote: imaginative, original, full of sock-you-in-the-eye brilliance, but most of it would be crap. And what did she get for it? A car that had to be push-started every night by a gang of loyal swains. "Seriously, though, Rodney, is it because of what your brother said?"

"When, miss?"

"Monday morning. Is it because of your father? If it is, that's just silly, isn't it? I can see why your father doing what he does might affect you – especially at your age. On the other hand..."

"It isn't that, miss," I said. "Honestly."

"Well, if it's because of this silly detective business, I think you've made a very big mistake, Rodney. You'll never make a detective. You need bigger feet and a much smaller head."

"How do you mean, miss?"

"Think about it, Rodney. On the other hand you *could* write me a lovely long mystery story."

"I'm well into my first case now, miss. And making progress."

"How interesting."

"I'm trying to find those missing dogs, miss."

"Charlotte told me."

"And," I said, "I think I've uncovered something worse."

"Oh?" This time she really did look interested. "It's not about that awful boy, is it?" she said.

"What awful boy, miss?"

"What's the matter, Rodney? He's not getting at you as well, is he?"

"Who, miss?"

"I'm not mentioning any names, but Mr Toogood's noticed a change since a certain person arrived. He's sure something nasty's going on, but it's hard pinning anything on a boy like that. I'd better be going."

"Want a hand to start your car, miss?"

"No, thank you, Mr Toogood's helping me tonight. I think he's man enough to manage on his own. And if I were you, Rodney, I'd give up the detective business. It doesn't look good for your health. But I *would* like you to write me something for the school magazine."

I hate disappointing adults, don't you? They're obviously so dependent on us for their happiness. But there are times when you have to put your foot down with a firm hand.

"Sorry, miss," I said.

I didn't go out of the front entrance that night. I *nearly* did. Then I remembered I'd left my zipper-jacket in the back porch. On the way there I saw Tarzan waffling along in his smelly football socks.

"Not coming to my practice, Penfold?" he said.

My soccer phase had lasted about a week. I'd quite liked the gear, I'd looked really good in it. I'd spent hours in front of the wardrobe mirror, heading imaginary balls on to the bed, and practising my poses.

"Not tonight, sir," I said. "I'm rather busy."

He grinned like a backward ape and went into his changing room.

Then, as I passed Mr Battrey's office, I witnessed something even smellier. You remember the red terminal? The one Mr Battrey had said contained all the really confidential material? Desmond Fiely was sitting in front of it, prodding keys like mad and looking scared to death behind his steamed-up specs. I was so shocked, I walked past without saying a word, and as I turned a corner I almost fell over his mum, who was on her hands and knees scrubbing the corridor.

"Hi, Rodney!" she said cheerfully. "How you going?"

I was so choked up I couldn't reply.

When I'd collected my jacket I walked round the outside of the school building – I felt I needed a breath of fresh air after what I'd just seen – and I was approaching the shed when I heard a voice say, "Let's see what's in your pockets. I'm feeling peckish."

A quiet, innocent voice: one I recognized at once.

"Shove off!" said a second voice from the shed, also one I knew.

"You want your face altering?" said Corvel.

"Get stuffed!" said Hamilton the Third.

I heard a lot of punches and scuffling. I could just imagine what was happening. I heard Corvel say, "Stop that! I'm warning you!"

I knew Hamilton wouldn't stand a chance. Byrne would be holding him, while Corvel did the hitting. I'd like to have gone round the corner of the shed and seized the despicable duo by the throats and thrust them up among the rafters – to a sticky end among the swallows' nests and worse.

But I didn't.

I stood there, listening. Wanting to do something. Not knowing what.

Then my quick brain did think of something.

I went to the front entrance and slipped quietly inside. With a bit of luck, Tarzan would still be in his changing room. Just before the interview for deputy head, he'd be pleased to nobble Corvel for bullying. It would practically clinch the job for him. I turned a corner and saw Tarzan swaggering out to join his hand-picked thugs; I was just about to call him back when an awful thought occurred to me. What if Tarzan, as a result of nobbling Corvel, *did* become deputy head? There flashed upon my inward eye a vision of every kid in the school hanging upside-down from the wall-bars, a pair of Tarzan's particularly pongy socks stuffed in his or her mouth, like something prepared for an awful feast.

I couldn't do that, not even to Desmond Fiely.

But what else could I do?

Then my brilliant brain thought of something else.

Remember the front entrance door? Remember the noise it made?

I retraced my steps till I was ten paces from the door; gathering all my considerable strength, I took a run and hit the door with all of my fifteen kilos. It really hurt my shoulder (I think I must have a very low Pain Threshold). But the door swung open with a convincingly Tarzan-like crash and I saw that success had crowned my endeavours.

Watching from behind the glass of the door, I saw Corvel, like a slimy rat, slipping through the railings into the park.

Hamilton the Third came round the corner of the shed and looked towards the door. I knew what was going through his tiny mind, though for some reason he wasn't looking half as chuffed as I thought he might be. I still didn't come out, in case Byrne was in the shed.

Hamilton went out of the gate and stood on the pavement, looking to his left. He took something out of his pocket and shoved it in his mouth. You have to admire the gall of a kid like that.

I came out of the door after a minute. He must have heard it sucking-to behind me, because he looked back. I started to walk towards him. I was going to tell him modestly how I'd rescued him, but just then a rust-bucket of a Mini drew up.

"Sorry I'm late, honey," I heard his mum say. "Machine got stuck."

"It's OK, Mum."

"You had a nice day? What's happened to your eye?"

"Ran into a wall," he said.

"You sure?"

"No sweat, Mum," he said.

She slung a bag of washing in the back as the kid climbed in. The door was nearly hanging off. It took him three goes to slam it shut. A moment later, they'd lurched off in a cloud of rust, and my chance of glory had gone.

I waited five minutes. Still Byrne didn't come out of the shed. I had to chance it. He wasn't there. I'd forgotten he was at the practice, of course. It was so nice to see a nice empty shed. He wasn't even hanging around in the rafters, upside down.

I went to the school gates and poked my nose round.

I could see Corvel talking to Harriet Far-laughn who was waiting at the bus stop. She normally looked white but now she looked an even paler shade of it.

I felt sorry for her. But what can you do?

I was glad when her bus came.

EIGHTEEN

On the way home I called in at Mr Patel's superstore. There were one or two questions I needed to ask. And it was exactly as I figured.

You remember the girl who'd been there when the cat food was stolen? The one wearing a blue dress? When I suggested to Mr Patel that it might have been a uniform, he nodded his head straight away.

"I think so, Rodney. It's possible."

"That's great, Mr Patel," I said. "Do you remember anything else about her? Did she have fair hair?"

"Fair hair, yes. You working for the police now, Rodney?"

He's a stocky little chap always ready for a joke. He was wearing a yellow T-shirt with a prisoner's number stamped on it.

"Did she have blue eyes, Mr Patel?"

"I think so, yes. And now you come to mention it, I don't remember this girl at the checkout counter. She must have gone out the back door. We had a lot of deliveries that day. And another funny thing. I remember her shopping bag was already heavy when she came in."

"That's great, Mr Patel," I said. "Thanks a

million!"

"Let me know if you don't find the culprit," he said, "and I'll see if I can get you promoted to Scotland Yard!"

When I got home, Oscar was sitting by the fridge, his enormous nose aimed at the door. My little brother was munching his way through the last banana, which is more or less his speciality.

Dad's mug and his toast were on the side, ready.

"Why don't you take it up for a change, Lester?" I asked.

"Mum said you had to."

"Why me again?"

He just looked at me.

"Where *is* Mum, anyhow?" I asked as I poured Dad's tea.

"She'll be back in a minute. She reckons another load of radioactive stuff is coming through tonight."

"What a laugh!" I said.

"Mum thinks it's serious."

"Talking of serious," I said, "you know your friend, Desmond? I saw him reading confidential files on the school computer tonight."

"I don't believe you."

"It's true."

He looked at me. "On the other hand," he said, "you could be right for once. Corvel was chatting him up after dinner."

"What about?"

"I couldn't hear but I think it's about Harriet."

"The trouble is," I said, "they're both scared as rabbits. It's no good being scared with Corvel."

For some reason Lester gave me one of his big looks.

"And why is that stupid dog looking at the fridge?" I asked.

"He thinks there's something in there. But there isn't. I've looked."

I put down the tray and opened the fridge door. I looked hard, but couldn't see a thing. Just olives and Perrier water, tomatoes and salad things. Oscar doesn't go much on those.

When I went up to my dad's study, he was staring out of the window. Staring, but not seeing anything.

I put the tray down on his desk, careful not to disturb his papers.

"Oh, it's you, son," he said. "Where's your mum?"

I told him.

"I wish she'd drop all this," he said. "She's getting herself agitated over nothing."

He took a sip of tea from his mug and tried to smile. He looked awful. Like an advert for dandruff and old age.

"What's up, Dad?" I asked. "Are you stuck?"

"Sort of, Rodney."

"Can't you get started?"

"Worse than that this time, son. I think I'm coming to the end of the Reverend Staystill."

The Rev. Staystill was this amateur detective my dad had been making a steady living from for years. Although his parish was in Lower Muddlecome – deep in the heart of Fiction County – and his twin passions those of butterflies and Commonwealth stamps, he managed to get involved in every crime for miles around. He was heavily into dandruff and paunch – a bit like Dad, really. But he always got his man, except in *Something Sharp and Nasty*, when it turned out to be a woman, a glamour puss on stiletto heels (which is the sole clue you need to find the murder weapon!).

"How about your own story?" Dad asked. "The one for Miss Quibble."

"I told you, Dad," I said, "I'm not really interested."

"You should try," he said. "I'm sure you'd do better than me. If I were you, I'd base the hero on yourself, Rodney. Just an ordinary kid. Maybe with a gang to help him. But don't make him too perfect."

"Good idea," I said, with as little enthusiasm as I could muster.

113

"Lester has been telling me that awful Eric Corvel has turned up again." You see what I mean about my little brother? "He's not bugging you, is he?"

"No, Dad."

"Let me know if he is and I'll come down and sort things out." He looked across at me. "Funnily enough, I went through a similar experience myself when I was at school. A kid called Claggerty."

"What happened?"

"Eventually I had it out with him. He whacked me, but it was a near thing. A lot nearer than I'd expected. I always had the feeling afterwards that if I hadn't waited for him to push me into it, things might have worked out differently."

"How do you mean, Dad?"

"If I'd made a decision. It might have given me – confidence – *something*. I don't know what."

I looked at him. The trouble with people who write stories for a living is that you can never tell whether they're telling the truth or not.

Most of the time they don't know themselves.

When I went downstairs, Oscar was still aiming his conk at the fridge and Mum was grabbing a sandwich. She looked worried as she switched on the telly.

"What's the matter, Mum?"

"We know for certain now, Rodney," she said. "The government's definitely bringing nuclear waste through."

"They wouldn't do a thing like that, Mum."

"They *are* doing it, Rodney."

Even my little brother, who was now starting on the last orange, looked sceptical. As it happened, the government minister materialized on the telly at that moment, as solidly reliable as a sago pudding. Anybody who doubted a man like that had to be deranged.

"Lies!" said my mother. "Lies! Lies! Lies!"

When I opened the fridge door to put Dad's milk away, I noticed something I hadn't seen before. A small tin of sardines, opened just a millionth of an inch.

"Boy, what a nose that dog has got!" I said, holding up the tin.

"I told you we should use him," said my little brother.

"Use him for what?" asked Mum as she pulled on her fur-lined boots.

"Finding the missing dogs. You know, this crime Rodney's supposed to be trying to solve. Oscar might be able to pick up the scent."

"Don't talk to me about crimes!" said Mum. "I'm off!"

A moment after she'd gone, Charlotte came in.

"You were right, Rodney," she said. "Lois *is*

going to join us after all. It was just like you said. She seemed interested as soon as I told her it wasn't Corvel we suspected. She says, will we call round for her tonight? And you'll never guess where she lives?"

"I don't have to guess," I said. "She lives at number eleven."

"But how did you know that?" asked Lester.

"Elementary, my dear Witless!" I said.

NINETEEN

I was pretty certain now who had the dogs. It was just a matter of nailing her. Charlotte wouldn't like that, of course. Neither would Lester – for obvious reasons! But that was just hard Cheddar on him.

When I phoned Mrs Wright, she said I had to come round before seven. She was going out later, she said; something about the new vicar at St Giles'. And when I phoned Mrs Verny's, it was Hamilton who answered.

"That you banging the school door tonight?" he said. "I just wanted to tell you about—"

I guessed he wanted to thank me so I cut him off short: I can't stand these embarrassing speeches of thanks.

"Forget it, Hamilton," I said modestly. "It was nothing. Listen. You doing anything special tonight?"

"Going down the gym later. Why?"

"Before that, could you just hang round the telephone? Say till we get round Mrs Verny's, in about an hour?"

"What for?"

"I want to know if a girl phones her. If she does, will you let me know? Say tip us a wink as we come in."

"OK."

"By the way, you ever see a Girl Guide round Mrs Verny's, Hamilton?"

"Maybe. What about it?"

"What was she like?"

Pause. "Dishy."

"It wasn't by any chance Lois DeWinter?" I said. "That new girl?"

"It could've been. I'm not sure. You don't really think it was her?"

"What do you mean?"

"Nicking Mrs Verny's dog."

"I never said that, Hamilton."

"It can't be her, man."

"You ever see this Girl Guide shopping for Mrs Verny? With a bag?"

"No," he said, after a pause. "What is this, man?"

"Never mind."

"You know Corvel was round again last night, scaring the old lady?" he said. "That's what you ought to be concentrating on. This time he got into her back yard. My brother scared him off. Which reminds me. You know when you banged the school door?"

I hadn't time for compliments. I told him I was in a hurry, and asked him to get Mrs Verny.

"OK," he said, "but we'll have to speak seriously about this later."

When Mrs Verny came to the phone she sounded shaky and worried.

"You all right, Mrs Verny? This is Rodney. I came round yesterday. With my brother and Charlotte."

"What you want now?"

"Has anything happened, Mrs Verny?"

"What about?"

I gave her time to think, then went on.

"Has your son been round to see you tonight, Mrs Verny?" I asked.

"I told you. He comes round every night."

"Half past six?"

"That's right."

"So could we come round before that, to see you?" I said.

"I suppose so."

"And you've nothing else to report?" I asked.

"What you mean? I'm sure I don't know what you're on about!"

As I put down the phone, I smiled. I hadn't expected her to mention Corvel knocking on her back door, of course. She'd probably still be far too scared to admit she'd even set eyes on him.

But I did think it funny she hadn't once mentioned her missing little dog.

TWENTY

Talking of dogs, I decided to take Oscar with us that night. Among other things, I suspected he might be interested in the scent on Charlie's famous red blanket. My little brother tried to claim the idea was his, of course, but you know what he's like by now.

"In any case," I said, "I bet the red blanket won't be there."

"What you mean, Rodney?" asked Charlotte.

"Mrs Verny's not playing straight by us," I said. "And I'll tell you something else: when we leave Lois's house, Lois won't come with us."

"You're horrible, Rodney!" Charlotte said.

"That's putting it mildly," said my little brother.

There was no sign of the Jaguar when we got there; just the imprint of its fat tyres on the gravel of the front garden.

I'd like to have pressed my nose against the basement window to see if the dogs were in there, but I didn't dare.

I rang the bell. Through the glass panels of the door we saw lights moving about in the hall beyond, and when the door opened I saw that they were candles. Otherwise the house was in darkness.

"Yes?" said Mrs DeWinter. Under the street-lamp she looked severe and gaunt. She wore a two-piece suit, black or dark blue, a white blouse with an ornate red bow at the neck, and high-heeled shoes (a bit like Camille de Clerke in *Something Sharp and Nasty*, to be honest). She didn't look pleased to see us, and particularly not to see Oscar.

"Hello, Mrs DeWinter," said Charlotte. "Is Lois in?"

Mrs DeWinter turned away from us. "Lois?" she called down the hall.

Beside her there was a state-of-the-art telephone on a small table; beyond her, five candles had been grouped on three consecutive treads of the stairs.

"Lois! Some friends of yours have called! And their dog!"

"I see you've no electricity yet, Mrs DeWinter," said Lester.

"That's right. These people are so awful."

"Are you going out for a meal, Mrs DeWinter?" asked Charlotte.

"That's right, darling. My taxi will be here any minute."

"Why don't you go in the Jag?" Lester asked.

"It's gone in for servicing," said Mrs DeWinter.

"Mother! Don't lie!" said Lois, who had

come out of the back room. Her blonde hair was bright in the light of the five candles on the stairs.

"Darling! How dare you speak to me like that!"

Lois didn't answer, just looked at her mother, shook her head as if in disbelief, then went back into the room.

"You'd better come in," Mrs DeWinter said at last when she'd more or less recovered. Even then her voice was unsteady.

We went down the hall and into the back room, Oscar leading the way. I'd made sure I was holding his lead, and wasn't surprised when he aimed his famous conk at the basement door by the kitchen. Nor did it surprise me that he went straight to Lois as we entered the room, and sniffed her hands, but I was disappointed that he sat beside her. Oscar is a dog of somewhat haughty disposition, normally stand-offish with new acquaintances. He was not like that with Lois.

"My mother is a terrible liar," she said as we came in. "We haven't got any electricity because we never paid the bills in our last house." She must have known her mother could hear every word. "And we haven't got the Jaguar because my dad's solicitors took it away this morning."

We were all too shocked to speak.

"Shall I close the door?" Charlotte said at last.

I felt Charlotte was right. I was the last one to enter the room and I closed the door. As I did so, Lois directed a mocking smile in my direction. She was sitting on what looked like a leather sofa, by the fireplace. There was no fire in the grate and the room was cold.

"If there's one thing I can't stand, it's a liar," said Lois, twiddling one of Oscar's ears (a liberty he doesn't usually permit). "My mother lies all the time. She can't help it. I hate her."

Even Lester seemed lost for words.

Again it was Charlotte who managed to reply.

"What's the matter, Lois?" she said. "You shouldn't hate your mum, no matter what she's done."

"She's a liar and a snob, and I hate liars and snobs, don't you?"

She seemed to look at me as she said this, and I almost said, *I do*. I stopped myself just in time. It would have sounded as if I were marrying her. But I was already warming to this girl, in spite of everything. The idea flashed through my mind that if anybody could deal with Corvel it was Lois DeWinter.

There were only two candles in the room, but my eyes were becoming accustomed to the dark now. There seemed to be very little furniture. I could see a standard lamp waiting for the great switch-on, and a posh dining table. It could have been genuine, or it could have been repro: I'm not deeply into furniture. Off to my right, there was a bookcase, half filled with books.

"Mind if I take a look at your books?" I said.

"Help yourself. They're all boring."

"We saw you in the yard," my brother said. She looked at him.

"Hitting Corvel," he explained.

"He's revolting. I don't like him."

"Nobody does," I said from over by the bookshelves.

I'd run my hand along the sofa back as I passed it. It was real leather. The books, though, were rubbish: mostly book club editions, backed in genuine imitation vinyl, the kind of books you bought to look good on a shelf and never read.

"Why doesn't somebody do something about him?" Lois asked.

"Some people are scared of him," said Lester, looking across at me.

"You're not scared of Corvel, are you?" she asked me. "You shouldn't be. You're a lot taller than him."

"And my mother's paid good money for him to have karate lessons," added Lester.

I pretended to be engrossed in a book called *The Art of Dinner Parties*.

"Was it nice at your other school?" Charlotte asked.

"Awful," said Lois. She turned back to me.

"I don't believe in being scared of people. You can easily blow people like Corvel away, if you have the guts to stand up to them."

Lester looked at her with adoring eyes, which was ridiculous, really, because only last week he'd had a passion for Miss Innocent's hamster.

"What is it about Corvel?" said Lois.

"What did he whisper in your ear, Lois?" I asked.

"Something horrible. I don't want to talk about it."

"That's what it is about Corvel," I said.

"Sticks and stones may break my bones," said Lois.

I know that's a saying even older than my dad, but I still don't believe it. Words *can* sometimes hurt you. Corvel's words can.

"Have you done karate lessons as well?" my little brother asked her.

"No."

"Not one lesson?"

"No."

"When you hit Corvel, you made a funny sound."

"That was just acting."

Interesting! I thought. I'd been right all along in suspecting somebody was acting a part at Mrs Wright's. It was just that I'd suspected the wrong actor.

"Were you scared?" asked Charlotte.

"Yes."

"You didn't look it," said Lester.

"I was," said Lois. "I just don't like being pushed around."

Oscar is a big dog. Sitting beside Lois, his jaws were more or less level with her head. If he'd wanted to he could have bitten it off. But even he was looking at her with adoring eyes now. She smiled at Lester. These two would be married soon (if Oscar didn't beat Lester to it) and I knew I had to act fast, before the gooeyness got out of hand.

"Can I ask a question?" I said. "Are you in the Girl Guides?"

"I used to be. Why?"

"You know this Mrs Wright who's had her dog nicked?"

"No."

"Well, if you went down to the bottom left hand corner of your garden and stepped over the fence, you'd be in hers. You can see her house from your kitchen. Last Saturday night she had a dog pinched, and we're trying to find it: she says a Girl Guide called at her house the night before."

"And you think it was me?"

"I didn't say that."

"It sounds like it, though! Are you scared to say what you mean?"

"That's the way he is," said Lester.

"In any case, my mother would never allow me to have a dog. Would you, Mother?" asked

Lois as her mother entered. "You don't like animals, do you? You think they're nasty, smelly things." She was twiddling Oscar's ears as she spoke.

"It isn't that, Lois..."

"They make messes, don't they, Mother? They don't *look* right."

"I really must be off now, darling," said Mrs DeWinter, drawing on her gloves. She didn't bend down to be kissed or anything like that. Just said a cold goodbye, to which Lois replied even more coldly.

I followed Mrs DeWinter out, closing the door behind me, and pretended I wanted to use the loo. As I'd hoped, she directed me to the downstairs one which – like the one in our house – is next to the internal door that leads to the basement. When she'd gone for her taxi, I tried the basement door. It was locked of course. But, when I rattled the door knob, and pressed my ear to the wood, I definitely heard something. A bowl being knocked over? A scratch? Something – or somebody – was down there.

I went in the loo, waited a moment, then pulled the chain.

Things looked really cosy when I rejoined the others.

"Find what you were looking for?" asked Lois.

"Maybe," I said. "I think there's somebody

– or something – in your basement, Lois."

"Do we have to go on like this, Rodney?" asked Charlotte.

"Don't worry about him, Lois," Lester said. "He can't help it."

"There *was* a tramp in our basement on Monday night," said Lois. "We let him stay the night, then we asked him to move on."

You could see the relief on Lester's face.

"And there's nothing in there now?" I asked.

"No."

"In that case, could we look?"

"I'm afraid we've lost the key," she said.

"Pity," I said. "And you don't know the other woman whose dog is missing – Mrs Verny? I don't suppose you've heard of her either?"

"No," said Lois. "I haven't."

"Mrs Verny denied knowing a Girl Guide when we asked her," I said, "but I don't think she was telling the truth."

"Let me get this straight," said Lois. "You think I put my Guide uniform on and nicked *both* these dogs now? Is that what you're saying?"

"I didn't say that. Anyhow, when I phoned Mrs Verny she didn't seem too worried about losing her dog – his name was Charlie, by the way. She never even mentioned him. I don't know why we bother. But I've brought Oscar tonight because I thought he might pick up Charlie's scent – from his old red blanket – when we go round to Mrs Verny's later."

"You're not accusing me of pinching the blanket as well?" said Lois.

"No, but you remember the day you came, the Head mentioned some shoplifting from Mr Patel's superstore?"

"As it happens, I don't."

"The point is," I said, "Mr Patel thinks that the girl who was there when the shoplifting happened might have been wearing a uniform."

"So you're accusing me of that as well now?"

She sounded indignant, but her gaze flickered for the first time.

"You haven't got Mrs Wright's dog?" I asked when I could manage it.

"No."

"In that case, why don't we all pop round to Mrs Wright's, and after that to Mrs Verny's, just for a chat?"

"Why not? Suits me," said Lois, standing up.

But she didn't come, of course. We got as far as the front door before she remembered her mum had asked her to stay in for a phone call.

"Tell you what, I'll see you up at Mrs Verny's, shall I?" she said.

"Fine by me," I said.

"Oh, by the way, where does Mrs Verny live?"

Charlotte told her.

Ha, blooming ha! I was thinking.

TWENTY-ONE

"What did I tell you?" I said when we were clear of the house.

"What's that supposed to mean?" asked Lester, as Oscar, in full sail, hauled him ahead towards his favourite niffy lamp-post.

"Ask yourself a simple question, Lester," I called after him. "Why hasn't Lois come with us to see Mrs Wright?"

"She *did* say she had to wait for a phone call," said Lester as Oscar brought him to a halt.

"She hasn't come because she doesn't want Mrs Wright to recognize her. Purely and simply that. And I'll tell you something else, Lester. She's probably making a phone call herself, at this very moment."

"Who to, Rodney?" asked Charlotte. "You mean to Mrs Wright?"

"No," I said, as we left Lester marooned behind us. "More likely to Mrs Verny."

"What sort of phone call?"

"I'm not really sure. But I bet we've seen the last of Lois tonight."

"Why are you so prejudiced against her?" asked Charlotte.

"It's you that's prejudiced, Charlotte," I said

patiently. "Remember what she said? *I'll see you up at Mrs Verny's*. How did she know it was up, not down? Or sideways?"

"She *was* at the assembly, Rodney."

"Yeah, but how does she know Omaney Road is *up*? I'll tell you how. Because she's already been to Mrs Verny's. *And* Mrs Wright's. I'm convinced she's the Guide who's been visiting both old ladies."

"Then why did she *admit* to being in the Guides?" asked Charlotte.

"A little bit of truth can often cover up a lot of lies," I said.

"She wasn't lying," said Lester, catching us up. "She didn't bat an eyelid the whole time. I was watching her."

"She batted both eyelids when I mentioned the shoplifting."

"*I* didn't notice."

"You wouldn't have noticed if she'd batted fourteen eyelids, Lester!"

"What's that supposed to mean?"

"You mean the candles?" said Charlotte.

"Partly the candles," I said.

"Candles? What you on about?" asked Lester.

"I thought you were the one with the big eyes?" I said. "How many candles were there in that room?"

"Four?"

"Two. And how come they had five candles

in the hall and only two in the living room, Lester?"

"Maybe they'd been watching TV before we came in," he suggested.

"With no electricity? No, they had only two candles in the room because Lois didn't want something to be seen in there."

"Like what?" asked Lester.

"Like her guilty face. Remember the moving lights we saw through the glass of the front door? That was Lois moving the candles out."

"I still don't believe Lois has nicked these dogs," said Lester.

"You wouldn't, Lester – and we all know why!"

"What do you mean by that?"

"Because you fancy her!"

"I don't!"

"Oh, stop arguing, you two!" said Charlotte. "Don't you believe anything Lois said, Rodney?"

"She was probably telling the truth about the Jaguar being taken away and her mother not paying the electricity bill," I said. "The rest of what she said I take with a tonne of salt. I'll bet a million pounds on one thing: by the time we get up to Mrs Verny's, that old red blanket of Charlie's will be missing. That's probably what Lois is phoning about. Telling her to get rid of it."

"But why?"

"Because she doesn't want Oscar to get its scent and find the dogs."

"You're crazy!" said my little brother. "Anybody ever told you?"

"If Charlie's blanket isn't there, that'll prove Lois is guilty."

"I don't see that," said Lester.

"If she turns up, will that prove she's innocent, Rodney?" asked Charlotte.

"It's a lot more complicated than that," I said.

"It would be!" said Lester.

As we turned the corner by the lights at the bottom of Vista Hill, I saw the tramp again, this time with a couple of his pals, even more trampy than him. He was leading them through the open doors of St Giles', just as if he owned it.

"I just know Lois hasn't nicked these dogs," said Lester, now being hauled ahead again.

"I think he's right, Rodney," said Charlotte.

"Well, we'll have to wait and see, won't we? Somehow, I think I'm going to enjoy tonight," I said, as Lester sailed round the corner into Park View Gardens at forty knots.

TWENTY-TWO

Mrs Wright almost had two fits when she saw Oscar.

"I don't allow Pagan to meet other dogs," she said. "They might have fleas. In any case, I don't think he'd like another dog in his house."

She was right: one glimpse of Oscar, and Pagan had collapsed on the carpet, feet up, and appeared to be passing himself off as dead.

"Oscar doesn't have to come in, Mrs Wright," I said. "My brother can take him round the side into your back garden, if that's OK?"

"Whatever for?"

"Just to test a theory."

"Oh, very well. You'll find the side gate unbolted," she told Lester, "but do be careful of my borders."

As Oscar and Lester retreated down the front steps, Pagan righted himself and growled.

"He's so brave!" Mrs Wright said as she closed the door behind Charlotte and me. "You haven't found my niece's dog, then?"

"Not yet," said Charlotte.

"What a pity. Sally will be so disappointed. You probably passed her in the street. She's been out for ages looking for the silly thing."

"I thought she wasn't coming till Friday night," said Charlotte.

"She wasn't. But she's so worried about that animal."

Mrs Wright steered us towards the kitchen; Pagan – his old self again now – triumphantly led the way.

Only one thing had changed in the kitchen since we'd last been. There were two cups on the table, instead of one. The fruit cake was still there; I wondered – doubtfully – if the niece had been offered a morsel.

"I do think it's a mistake to become so dependant on an animal, don't you?" said Mrs Wright, breaking off a piece of cake and stooping down to pop it in Pagan's mouth. "Sally is so silly about these things."

"Is she staying the night with you?" asked Charlotte.

"The BBC need her for something special tonight. She's coming back Friday night, though, and she'll be staying the weekend."

"She must be keen," said Charlotte.

"She so enjoys coming here," said Mrs Wright.

I was just wondering what kind of girl it was who enjoyed staying with Mrs Wright, when from the garden we heard Oscar give one of his curious honking barks: Mrs Wright hurried to the window.

"I do hope your dog doesn't make a mess on my lawn," she said.

Joining her at the window, I saw Oscar going round and round and round the lawn, like some grotesque mechanical toy gone wonky. Lester, behind, was only just managing to hang on.

"I think I'd better help my little brother," I said.

"Good idea," said Mrs Wright. "But do watch my borders."

As I descended the steps by the back door I noticed that the cardboard box and bit of mattress had been removed. Not that it mattered: Oscar seemed to have caught Bess's scent. Tail up, nose down to the ground, he was now heading straight for the Middletons' garden.

By the time I caught up with them and grasped the lead, Oscar was moving so fast that we went through the Middletons' hedge backwards.

"What's happening?" asked Lester, as we emerged on the other side.

"Maybe you fed him too much meat," I said.

We crossed the Middletons' lawn like the Spanish Armada in full sail and seconds later scudded across the grass of number eleven. Oscar dropped anchor by number eleven's basement window.

We couldn't see a thing down there, but Oscar was whining, and that told me all I wanted to know. I only hoped Lois hadn't seen us. I had seen no sign of her as we were hauled across the lawn, but that didn't mean a lot in a darkened house.

I told Lester to pull Oscar back while I bent down to the window: "Bess!" I called. "Are you there, Bess?"

There was a low woof accompanied by the barking of a smaller dog.

I looked up at Lester when I heard that.

"It might not be Lois," he said. "She might not know anything about it." But he didn't believe his own words. "It might not even be the dogs we're looking for," he said.

I surprised him by agreeing. He almost smiled. "Tell you what," I said, "till we're absolutely certain, we won't say a word of this to anyone. OK?"

"You're right, Rodney," he said.

I think it was the first time he'd agreed with me about anything, since he had been in nappies.

Half-way back to the traffic lights, we met Mrs Wright's niece. I saw her coming towards us and guessed who she was at once. She was a slim, attractive girl, but under the street lights she looked pale and worried.

"Excuse me," I said. "Are you Mrs Wright's niece?"

"How did you know? Are you the children

who are helping to find Bess? You haven't found her yet?"

"Not yet," I said. She looked so disappointed when I said that. Her face seemed to crumple. For a moment, I thought she might even cry. Quickly, I added, "But I think we may be on her trail."

Sally's face brightened at once. If Mrs Wright couldn't see why her niece needed a dog, she could never have looked really closely. I could see that Sally was lonely. I could understand why she so enjoyed staying with her aunt: even if that aunt was Mrs Wright.

"We're not one hundred per cent sure," I said. "But we might have some news pretty soon. We certainly hope so."

"I'd be so grateful," said Sally.

"Is it an important programme you're doing tonight?" asked Charlotte.

"Programme?"

"Mrs Wright said it was something special. She told us you were really important. At the BBC."

"I do work at the BBC," she said, "but I'm not important. I work in the kitchens. I'm a glorified washer-upper, really. I'm learning to do catering." She bit her lip.

"Maybe you *will* be important one day," said Lester.

"I doubt it." She shook her head. "I'm sorry

Aunty Stella gave you the wrong impression. Aunty Stella is a bit like that. She likes to give people the idea that..." Her voice tailed off.

"That she's more important than she is?" said Lester. "Don't worry, we have somebody in our family like that."

And he looked straight at me as he spoke.

TWENTY-THREE

All the same, I was feeling pretty chuffed as we said goodbye to Mrs Wright's niece. I knew now where both dogs were. And, though I was still in the dark about her motives, I was pretty certain who'd taken them.

"You know something we don't, Rodney?" Charlotte asked.

"He thinks he does!" said Lester. "He thinks he knows everything!"

The church clock was striking half past six as we crossed at the lights. The rent-a-mob was already on parade, the tramp in the thick of it – next to my mother, as it happened. A lot of them were holding up silly posters saying DON'T TURN BRITAIN INTO A NUCLEAR DUSTBIN! which I personally thought was a load of rubbish.

Hamilton was waiting for me half-way up Vista Hill. He tipped me a wink so subtle that somebody setting off from Land's End in thick fog could have seen it. I wandered over to him.

"You was right," he said. "That new girl did phone. It still don't prove nothing, though."

"What she say?"

"What you think I am, man, a spy? Tell you

what, though, I reckon Corvel is on to her about something."

"How d'you mean?"

"She crossed over at the lights not ten minutes ago, I think heading for Mrs Verny's, but Corvel come out of the cemetery and stopped her."

"The cemetery?"

"He's always in there now. Don't you know? He'd been talking to Desmond. That other kid was with him, the one with a face like something a bus has run into."

"Byrne, you mean?"

"Desmond was telling Corvel something. Then, when Lois come, Corvel went straight over to her and said something in her ear, just like he done in school. Only this time it was different. She went dead white."

"You sure?"

"She turned round and crossed straight back over the road when the lights was against her. She could've been killed, easy. Then that new vicar run out to stop the traffic. She was in a right panic."

"What new vicar?" I said.

He turned round. "He was there a minute ago," he said. I noticed that half a dozen mob members, including my mother and the tramp, had gone. "He must've gone back in the church. Which reminds me... On the phone I wasn't telling you the truth. I *had* seen Lois going shopping for the old lady. I admit it now."

"You didn't notice if her bag was heavy, did you?"

He hesitated only a second. "It was. But I still reckon it isn't her."

"Thanks a lot, Hamilton. You off to the gym now?"

"Later. That reminds me of something else. Thanks a million for ruining my fight with Corvel. I was just whopping him real good when you went and banged that door."

"You were beating Corvel?"

"Sure I was, man. What's the matter with you? I know he give me this black eye, but that's nothing. You should've seen *his* eyes! There was fear in them, man, I saw it. He was real scared. He won't lay a finger on me again, or he'll get this." And once more he demonstrated his amazing straight left.

"Sorry about that, Hamilton. Before you go, how about one more small favour?"

"What you think I am, man? A messenger boy or something?"

"We're just going to see Mrs Verny. Could you hang about for say half an hour and, if you do happen to see Corvel wandering up in her direction, give us a warning?"

"What you want me to do?"

"You're a pal, Hamilton. Just buzz her buzzer three times. OK? Three times."

TWENTY-FOUR

Mrs Verny made a big fuss of Oscar as she let us in, even though he was putting on his Lord Snooty look. Then she made a show of looking round for Charlie, as if I'd hidden him in my back pocket.

"So you haven't found my little Charlie, yet?" she asked. "I thought you might have by now. I've been so worried!"

Hamilton's big brother was draped over the banister again, like something bad and broody on a film-set. I saw I'd been wrong about the message to the world on his T-shirt. It didn't actually say I MAKE TROUBLE but I MAKE MUSCLE, not that that made any difference: I knew that plenty of our modern-day criminals spend their time in prison building up their bodies so they can bop bank clerks more effectively when they finally get released.

"These kids not giving you any hassle, are they, Mrs Verny?" he said as we passed below him.

"No, thanks, Mr DeFreitas," she said, smiling up.

"That's OK, then. Just let me know if you need any assistance."

Assistance! What a blooming cheek! I thought.

"He's nice," said Mrs Verny to us as we went in her room. "They're all nice upstairs. Lot nicer than I thought."

"The police still calling for him?" I asked when the door was shut.

"Yes, but I can't believe he's done anything really bad."

"Where's Tiddles, Mrs Verny?" asked Charlotte.

"In the cupboard, dear. You can let her out if you like."

Of course, the first thing I looked for was Charlie's red blanket. I wasn't surprised to see it had gone. After all, that was what Lois had been ringing Mrs Verny about.

I was glad the chain was on the back door. I didn't want Corvel bursting in on us. It was a pity, though, that the curtains weren't drawn, either over the window or the glass panels of the door. I wandered towards the fireplace and saw – to my great disappointment – that my little brother had been right about the photographs on the mantelpiece: there was no picture of her son. Lester saw me looking, and a self-satisfied smirk came over his face. Mrs Verny's clock was still almost three-quarters of an hour slow, which meant that her precious son – if he existed at all – should have been here yonks ago.

"Has your son been to visit you today, Mrs Verny?" I asked.

She glanced at the clock, which showed twenty-five past six. "No," she said as she settled into her chair, "but he'll be here presently."

The kitten strutted out as soon as Charlotte opened the cupboard door. Charlotte tried to pick her up, but she still didn't want to be held. She delivered one of her stupendous *Sptttts!* and walked arch-backed over to Oscar, who looked the other way and pretended to study the wallpaper. It was ridiculous, really, such a big animal being scared by such a small bundle of fluff. Then Tiddles rubbed herself against Mrs Verny's crumpled stocking and sat down in front of the fire, her back to Oscar, totally ignoring him.

"You shouldn't really keep Tiddles in a cupboard, Mrs Verny," said Charlotte. "I don't think she likes it."

"I have my reasons," said Mrs Verny.

"I just wish you'd tell us them," I said. "You know that Girl Guide we told you about? She hasn't been round to see you yet?"

"I told you! No Girl Guides have ever been in this house."

It was a sad moment for me. I was sorry for Mrs Verny with her twisted stockings and her toes sprouting through her slippers. But she was lying about the Girl Guide (who I now knew for certain was Lois DeWinter), just as she had been all along about her fictitious son. I wanted to help her. We all did. But how can you help people when they won't tell you the truth?

"There *was* something else I wanted to tell you," she said.

"What's that, Mrs Verny?" asked Charlotte.

"It's about them boys that's been to see me," she started to say. But at that moment her front door buzzer buzzed.

Mrs Verny's face went white.

"Whoever can that be?" she said. "At this hour?" (She'd forgotten, of course, that it should have been her son.)

"I think it's just a friend of ours, Mrs Verny," said Charlotte.

I hoped she was right. There had been only two buzzes, but it could still mean Corvel. It was always possible Hamilton had forgotten his promise to sound the alarm and had wandered off, drawn by the pull of the punchbag and the pong of the gym. You can't always trust other people.

"Will you see who it is, Rodney?" said Charlotte, smiling.

It was Lois.

Looking decidedly uneasy. And Mrs Verny wasn't looking exactly natural when I did the introductions.

"Sorry, I didn't quite catch your name, dear?"

"Lois," said Lois, dutifully.

"I don't think I've ever met a Lois before," said Mrs Verny.

What an act it all was! It was just a pity for them that Tiddles ran up to Lois and purred against her leg.

"And you're going to help these children find my little dog, are you, Lois?" said Mrs Verny as she sat down in her chair again. (I wondered how she knew that: *we* certainly hadn't told her.)

"That's right, Mrs Verny," said Charlotte. "What was it that you were going to tell us just now?" She turned to Lois. "Mrs Verny was just telling us about some boys who've been calling on her," she explained.

"Oh?" said Lois. "That sounds interesting." She sat on the chair opposite Mrs Verny. "Who was that, Mrs Verny?"

"I should've told you before," said Mrs Verny, turning to me. "Them two boys I told you about. I wasn't being entirely honest. It was wrong of me."

"What were these two boys like, Mrs Verny?" asked Lois.

"One was a big tough boy. But he wasn't the worst. The other was smaller. Fair hair. Blue eyes. First time I saw him I thought, *There's a proper little angel.* But I was wrong."

"What did they do, Mrs Verny?" I asked.

"At first I thought they was nice. They just said they wanted to take Charlie for a walk, and I let them. When they come back they said they wanted money, so I give them some."

"A lot?"

"Just pennies at first. It was lucky Tiddles was out hunting, that first night. They never knew about her."

"Then what happened?" I asked.

"They come back again the next night. They said something might happen to Charlie if I didn't give them more money. Charlie didn't want to go with them, I could see that. I knew they'd been badly using him, but I had to let him go, I was that frightened."

"And did they bring him back?"

"Yes."

"And you gave them more money?"

"I had to."

"How much?"

"In the end I was givin' them pounds. I couldn't really afford it. That's why it had to stop."

"Then what happened? Do you think they've got Charlie now?"

"I never said that." She glanced at Lois. "Like I told you, he just went out one night and never come back." We all saw Lois go pink. (This room wasn't lit by just two candles.) In what I took to be a further telling piece of evidence, Tiddles jumped on to her lap and began purring up into her face, as if comforting her. "I don't want no trouble," said Mrs Verny.

"Listen, Mrs Verny," I said. "We think we know who these boys are."

"Do you? Well why don't you report them?"

"We're ninety per cent certain. If we got you up to school, would you identify them? You're the only one who can do it."

"Oh, I couldn't do that, dear."

"The point is this, Mrs Verny," I said, "it's no good being scared of boys like these, is it? The more scared you are, the worse they get. They'll go on getting more and more money out of you. Out of other old people as well. Somebody has to take a stand against them."

"Maybe she's too scared, Rodney," said Lester. "Some people are."

Lois nodded and looked across at me.

"Is that why you keep Tiddles locked in the cupboard, Mrs Verny?" asked Charlotte.

"That's right, dear. I don't want them taking her as well."

"So you *do* think they have Charlie?" I said.

"I never said that. I get confused. Last night, they come round again. They tried to get in through that back door. They was saying things, horrible things. Horrible, wicked things. Then Mr DeFreitas up there shouted, and they ran away. I get that frightened."

"Don't be," said Charlotte. She went to Mrs Verny and put her arm round her. "We'll look after you, won't we, Rodney?"

When Charlotte looks at me like that my knees sort of melt.

"Sure," I said. "Sure we will."

"Mrs Verny?" said Charlotte. "You have got enough money to feed Tiddles, have you? We can lend you some if you like."

"That's kind of you, but I always keep plenty of tins under the sink."

I went to the sink and opened the doors beneath it. She was telling the truth this time. There were seven tins of cat food in there, as well as some cat biscuits.

"I see there's no dog food, Mrs Verny," I said.

"I always fed Charlie on cat food," she said. "It's got more meat in it. I heard on the news some poor woman's been living on it round here."

Desmond flipping Fiely strikes again! I thought.

"That's fine," I said.

There was a silence during which we could hear the steady thump-thump of music from upstairs.

"You sure you don't want Rodney to speak to the people upstairs, Mrs Verny?" Charlotte said. "You wouldn't mind, would you, Rodney?"

"'Course not!" I said, knees knocking. "Why should I?"

"They're all right," said Mrs Verny. "The noise is company."

And then we heard another noise.

A noise that wasn't company.

The noise of the front door buzzer. Once. Twice. A third time.

TWENTY-FIVE

"Corvel's on his way!" I said.

I expected him to try the front door first, but of course he was too clever for that. It was just lucky for all of us that by the time we heard him scrambling over the back-yard wall, Lois had already switched out the light and drawn the curtains over the window and the door. Which, all things considered, I thought was pretty smart of her.

I don't know how long we sat there in the dark. Hardly moving, scarcely breathing.

"Old lady?" Corvel said. "You in there?" He sounded as if his mouth were pressed against the lock of the door. He rattled the handle. The key was in its normal place, hanging from its hook on the door-jamb: he had only to break a pane of glass and he could reach it. "I *know* you're in there," he said.

He probably did know: he could probably *see*. That feeling I'd had at my old junior school, about him knowing everything: I'd never really shaken it off.

"Why don't you open the door, old lady? All I want to do is talk. Can you hear me?" He tried the handle again, harder this time; gave the door a push, made it shake. "You got the shoplifter in there with you again, old lady? You know she's a shoplifter?"

Lois lowered her head over Tiddles, who was the only one of us not scared (Oscar was terrified), but not before I glimpsed her face. The fire threw a warm lively light over her features, but by now they were tired and frozen and dead. This was the face of a frightened person. And I knew why Lois was scared.

I also knew that somebody, sometime, had to break out of this web of fear we were all of us bound up in.

And I knew who that person had to be. Unfortunately.

"Open the door, old lady. I might get nasty if you don't let me in. You hear me? Something might happen to your dog."

Mrs Verny glanced at Lois when he said that and Lois lifted her head and tried to smile. She reached out and placed her hand reassuringly on Mrs Verny's.

That was the moment when I finally understood about Lois DeWinter. That small gesture of comfort – with Tiddles already on her lap and Oscar cowering under her skirts – allowed me finally to see the light.

"I don't want no money, old lady. Just a nice friendly talk."

That was all Corvel ever wanted. I remembered all the nice friendly talks we used to have at my old school. I remembered that first day when he'd laughed as he watched me pee in my pants.

"Old lady? Why don't you open the door?"

How long was this going to go on? I wondered. How long were we going to sit in the dark, holding our breath, pretending we weren't there? I remembered my dad's story (Was it a story?) about the bully at his school. I didn't want a busted nose. On the other hand, I didn't want to pee in my pants all my life...

"Old lady? I know you're in there."

He shook the door again. Buffeted it. I thought the glass panels would break. Some of the neighbours must have heard. But nobody came.

Tiddles made one of her *Sptttz* noises, and growled.

"You got a cat, old lady? You never told us about that! You naughty old lady! You haven't had that DeWinter girl pinching cat food for you? I bet the police would like to hear about that! Pussy! Pussy! Come to me!"

Tiddles sprang down from Lois's knee and went to the door, spitting fury.

"I'd really like to see your cat, old lady. Tell you what I'll do: come back another night, shall I, when you're in? That suit you? I'd love to see your little cat! Give it a bit of discipline!"

He laughed. He thumped the door again.

Mrs Verny sobbed aloud.

He must have heard because the buffeting stopped.

I almost acted then. I almost bounced out of my chair and unlocked the door and confronted him. But what good would that really have done? As my dad often said about his stories, timing was all.

And it was a good job I hesitated.

Because a moment later we heard Hamilton's outsize brother roar something extremely rude from the window above, and a moment after that Corvel had scarpered back over the yard wall so fast he can hardly have touched the bricks.

TWENTY-SIX

Tiddles was the first to recover: she leapt back on to Lois's lap and mewed. Poor Oscar was still in a state of shock.

"That boy's evil," said Mrs Verny, her voice shaking. "And what for's he telling all them lies about you shoplifting, Lois?"

Lois didn't reply.

"Because he's a liar," I said. But I suspected that when Corvel had accused Lois of shoplifting he was probably speaking the truth.

"Proper evil," said Mrs Verny. "Somebody ought to do something."

"Don't worry, Mrs Verny," said Lester, "my big brother's going to fix him, aren't you, Rodney?"

"He *wants* fixing, good and proper," said Mrs Verny.

I cleared my throat.

"If it's any consolation, Mrs Verny," I said, "I don't think you need to worry about Charlie."

"What do you mean by that?"

"I'm pretty sure I know where he is."

I noticed Lois's face got some of its colour back as I spoke.

"Do you?" asked Mrs Verny. "Where?"

"I don't think you know about Mrs Wright," I said, "but her niece has lost *her* dog as well, and I think both dogs are in the same place."

"Oh? And where exactly would that be, dear?"

"I can't tell you that just yet, Mrs Verny," I said. "But I don't think Charlie is in any danger, not at the moment."

"I must say this sounds very funny –" started Mrs Verny. She must have realized how unconvincing she sounded because she stopped. "Still," she said, "I suppose it's all right as long as that boy hasn't got him."

"He hasn't," I said. "I think both dogs are in capable hands. You might even say *loving* hands."

Lois looked up then, looked me straight in the eye. I think she knew exactly what was going through my mind: that I knew not only about her and the dogs but also about Corvel and her. Oscar, now almost recovered, lifted his head from her lap to give me an approving glance.

"On the way here, we met Mrs Wright's niece," said Charlotte to Lois. "Looking for her dog." I think Charlotte was trying to relieve the tension, but she only made matters worse as far as Lois was concerned.

"Are you sure?" said Lois, the words rushing out. "I thought her niece wasn't supposed to come till Friday? Is she staying the night?"

"No," said Lester. "Why?"

"But guess what, Lois," I said, not wanting to keep her in misery. "Her niece is *coming back* on Friday to look for her dog again."

"Is she?" said Lois, relief written all over her face.

"I must say, that is good news," said Mrs Verny, glancing at Lois.

"Shall I make you a cup of tea, Mrs Verny?" asked Charlotte.

"That would be nice, dear. I still feel all of a shake." She glanced at the clock. "I can't think what's kept my son. He should have been here long since."

I didn't want to upset Mrs Verny any further, but if we were really going to help her, we'd all have to start telling the truth.

"Excuse me, Mrs Verny," I said, "but would you mind if I asked you a question about your son? Something you might not want me to ask?"

As Charlotte poured boiling water over the tea-bag she gave me one of her this-is-what-I'd-like-to-do-to-you glances. Mrs Verny just looked worried.

"I'm sorry if I'm wrong," I said, "but I don't think you have a son, Mrs Verny. Have you?"

She looked across at Lois who bent down her head to Oscar.

"No," she said. "That was another lie I told

you. I do hope the Good Lord will forgive me."

"Don't worry," I said. "I'm sure He will."

"My brother's a personal friend," explained Lester.

"What I mean is," I said, "*we*'ll certainly forgive you, Mrs Verny."

"Hear hear," said Charlotte.

"You made up the story of the big strong son to scare off Corvel, didn't you, Mrs Verny? And you thought we were his friends?"

"That's right."

"Never mind, Mrs Verny," said Charlotte, handing her the cup of tea and looking at me like poison.

I allowed her to have a sip of tea before I asked, "Getting back to Charlie, Mrs Verny, do you really think he's lost?"

"Whatever do you mean by that?" Her teacup rattled in its saucer. "'Course I've lost my dog! You think I'd send a message to the school if I hadn't?"

"OK," I said. "I'm sorry."

Charlotte was glaring at me by now. "You really are stupid sometimes, Rodney."

"Sorry," I said. I let Mrs Verny compose herself before asking, "You know that old red blanket of Charlie's?"

A slight hesitation.

"What about it? I'm tired of answering all these questions."

"I noticed it isn't by the back door any

more. It's just that if we're going to find Charlie, it might help if Oscar picked up his scent. So could he just smell the blanket? Do you happen to know where it is?"

"I'm sure I can't think where I've put it," said Mrs Verny. "I looked this morning for it, but it wasn't there. I can't think what I've done with it. I must have thrown it out. I must be getting funny in me old age!"

Which was exactly the answer I was expecting.

"It doesn't matter," I said. "It isn't really important any more."

TWENTY-SEVEN

It didn't surprise me that when we left, Lois stayed behind to talk with Mrs Verny: I suspected those two had a lot to discuss.

I opened the front door just a speck before I poked my nose out. But there was no sign of Corvel.

Across the street, though, gazing down from an upstairs window, I saw the worried face of the Squit. I hadn't realized that he lived opposite Mrs Verny. I guessed that Corvel must have been squeezing information out of the poor kid about vulnerable Mrs Verny.

I smiled at him to show that there were no hard feelings. He stepped away from the window, as if afraid.

For some reason, there was no traffic surging up or down Vista Hill. Not a single vehicle. And when I poked my nose further out I saw the worrying twinkle of blue patrol cars down by the lights.

Hamilton explained when we met him halfway down the hill: "Some sort of accident, man. A big lorry got out of control and whammed into another one. They've hit the safety barrier. There's an awful pong down there. I'm going to tell my brother so he can get in on it."

"Thanks for buzzing the buzzer, Hamilton," I said. "You know your brother scared Corvel off again?"

"He'd enjoy that. He likes bossing people around. Been trying to boss me around since I was born, but I just give him one of these," and he delivered two of his famous straight lefts into solid air. "That Corvel guy read your mind or what?"

"How do you mean?"

"Soon as he come out of the alley he started mouthing off at me. Accused me of warning Mrs Verny. Cheek! He couldn't even have seen me."

"What did you say?"

"Told him to get stuffed. So then he said he was setting his pet gorilla on me tomorrow morning. So then I told him to stuff it where the monkey shoves its nuts."

"What exactly does that expression mean?" asked Charlotte.

"I've never been sure, Charlotte," I said, "but I suspect it could be rude." I turned to Hamilton. "What are you going to do? Stay off school?"

"Not me, man. I'm not scared of them. No way!"

"Why don't you tell your big brother?"

"No good. He's in court tomorrow."

"Is he in big trouble?" I asked.

"What you on about, man? My brother's joining the police force! He's just started his training. What you think he is? Some kind of criminal or something? You're crazy, man! Anyhow, I'll handle this myself."

He punched air again, most impressively.

"So you're just going to turn up for a thrashing tomorrow?" I said.

"Might as well. Then I can enjoy the rest of the day."

He grinned at me, then hurried on up the street.

"What are you going to do?" Charlotte asked me.

"Me?" I said. "Do? What about?"

"About Hamilton," she said. "About Mrs Verny. About everything." And again she smiled at me in that particular kind of way that makes my bones go runny. "You know you're the only one who can do anything about it, Rodney, don't you?"

I had to admit that was true.

"Just be patient," I told her. "Soon I'll fix everything."

"Oh yeah?" said Lester. He also said something else – by the look on his face, probably something sarcastic. But luckily at that moment a fire-engine thundered obligingly downhill, and drowned out his words.

* * *

By the time we reached the bottom of Vista Hill, it was hard to see what all the fuss had been about. The two lorries had been dragged away, and the only remaining evidence of an accident was a slight dent in the safety barrier and a small patch of something which had been spilled on the road ... something which seemed to be burning a hole through the tar.

In the days which followed, that small patch of Something proved to be very important. Maybe I should have realized its importance at the time – from the swarms of police and the fact that the firemen were wearing masks as they sprayed the road – but I didn't. These things seemed dull and routine, and my attention was drawn by other things.

There must have been over a hundred protesters by now, some of them local people, including Mr Patel. The tramp, red-faced, was at the front, shouting louder than any of them. I guessed he was drunk. On one side of him was my mother and on the other, Mrs Wright. I only hoped, for all our sakes, he didn't have fleas. Just then a posh car drove up and a chap got out. At first I didn't recognize him. He didn't look quite the same as he had done on the telly. But it was the government minister all right. As he strode towards the police, he patted the hanky neatly folded in his breast pocket. He tried to smile, but he didn't look so confident now: if you looked beyond the expensive suit and that folded hanky, you could see he was frightened.

"Hurry along," the policeman said to us as we crossed the road. (Oscar growled.) "It's all over now. Nothing to worry about. Keep moving."

We kept moving. Somewhere in the huddle of firemen, I had heard the click-click-click of that instrument they use to measure radioactivity, and looking back I saw that the minister was being helped into some special overalls and a respirator. More police had arrived in a van, some of them with big plastic helmets and big batons: the sort of police I had seen only on the telly, in other peoples' capitals, where the citizens get out of control. The protesters pressed forward, my mother and the tramp at the front.

"I bet he hasn't a clue what's going on," I said when we reached the other side and looked back.

"Who?" said Charlotte.

"Blackbeard," I said. "The tramp."

"Him?" she said. "He isn't a tramp, Rodney."

"Who is he, then?"

"That's the new vicar of St Giles'," said Lester. "Didn't you know?"

For a moment I was speechless.

"When did you find that out?" I said.

"Desmond told me yesterday."

"It's true, Rodney," said Charlotte. "Never mind."

"To be honest, big brother," said Lester, "I don't think this detective business suits you. You better give up!"

"Not just yet," I said. "Not just yet."

"What do you mean, Rodney?" asked Charlotte.

"Tonight I picked up some valuable clues at Mrs Verny's."

"Like what?" asked my little brother.

"Like, for instance, how did Lois know Mrs Wright's niece wasn't supposed to come till Friday? Did either of you tell her that?"

"That doesn't prove anything," said Lester.

"And why did Mrs Verny say it was a relief that the niece was coming back on Friday? What's she supposed to know about it?"

"Huh!" said Lester.

"Also," I said, "I'm certain now who did the shoplifting."

"You don't still think it was Lois, Rodney?" asked Charlotte. "You can't believe what Corvel said!"

I didn't answer that.

"He does!" said Lester. "He really does! Just look at his face!"

"Do you, Rodney?"

I still didn't answer. Instead, I smiled wryly.

"In Dad's books, the Reverend Staystill always unravels the mystery to an assembled audience in Colonel Clutterbuck's library or Lady Boring's withdrawing room. Usually on page 182. And that's exactly what I'm going to do."

"What do you mean, Rodney?" asked Charlotte.

"Tomorrow," I said, "by the murky light of Lois's back room, all shall be revealed."

"Oh yeah?" said my little brother.

"Oh yeah, oh yeah, oh yeah, little brother!" I replied.

TWENTY-EIGHT

I didn't sleep much that night. I lay awake listening to Oscar and my insensitive little brother snoring in unison. I watched the blink of police lights on our bedroom wall. I heard Mum come home in the small hours of the morning – and heard her and Dad talking for ages down in the kitchen.

I couldn't face breakfast. But at least Mum didn't nag this time; her mind was on higher things. She was sporting, with pride, the bump on her brow bestowed by the riot police, and her eyes were glued to the telly where the government minister was announcing his resignation. It was true, he said, that he hadn't been entirely honest in his earlier interviews, but he had always acted in the best interests of national security. He'd done nothing he was ashamed of, he said.

"So you were right all the time," Dad said to Mum. He looked awful. After Mum had gone to bed, he'd stayed up all night completing what was to be the last of the Staystill mysteries. "Want another cup of tea?"

Mum nodded and smiled. After *her* action-packed night she looked younger somehow, more bright-eyed and bushy-tailed.

"What happens next?" Dad said as he re-filled her cup.

"We're having a meeting this morning," she said. "To consider what we should do. It isn't the end, you know."

"No, I didn't think it would be. Ends have a habit of turning into beginnings; I know that. And this time I think I'll join you. OK?"

Which made Mum smile even more.

I can't say that I was smiling as I went into the school yard. I wasn't at all sure I could carry my plan through.

The first bit was easy, though. I caught Desmond Fiely as he stepped into the yard, and told him I wanted a word: "About reading personal files," I said.

"What you on about?"

"I'm on about Lois DeWinter."

"You're nuts!"

"You got into her personal file last night, Desmond," I said. "And then told Corvel about it."

He almost collapsed on the playground.

"Listen, Desmond," I said. "I'm on your side. I know why you're running around for Corvel: to protect Harriet. She's terrified of him, isn't she? He's got her dumping litter in people's front gardens, hasn't he? Is he shaking money out of her? Whatever it is, it's no use giving in to Corvel. We have to try something else... Will you help me, Desmond? I *need* your help. I need a lot of people's help. I just want you to do something not so very different from what you do every day. Say yes?"

He didn't look too happy. He shook his head.

"Get this straight, Desmond," I said. "Whether my plan works or not, the Head is going to find out what Corvel has been up to. What Corvel has been up to *with your help*. So you might as well come out of this smelling of roses, instead of the other stuff."

"What you want me to do?"

When I told him, he went pale.

"But what if Byrne doesn't believe me?"

"He'll have to," I said. "If he doesn't, my plan won't work. Then we'll all be for it. Including Harriet."

He nodded then. Not too enthusiastically. But at least he nodded.

A minute later, I caught Hamilton as he baled out of the rust buggy. I explained what his job was.

"That all?" he asked. "You don't want me to play a more active part?" And once more he demonstrated that straight left.

"I think I'm man enough to do this on my own, Hamilton," I said.

"You're crazy. You seen too many films!"

"You and all your undersized associates come in only if the Byrne plan fails," I said.

"It's your funeral," he said, which I thought a bit near the bone.

As I crossed the yard, I saw Lester looking at me in a way he'd never done before. I'd given him his instructions already, and he must have been talking to Charlotte, because she was looking in my direction, fairly full-up of awe. The poor girl had always doted on me, of course, but this was pure hero worship.

TWENTY-NINE

As I went down the final corridor two first years bolted out of the bogs and shot past me like frightened rabbits, their ears flat back and their fur sticking up with fear. By now Desmond was in his usual position, pretending to read the notices.

"Don't forget, Desmond," I said. "One minute."

"What if he won't come out?"

"Tell him they're thinking of making him a prefect."

"He'll never believe that!"

"Just try him," I said.

Corvel had the Squit in a cubicle when I went in. Byrne was laughing as he watched what Corvel was doing. It wasn't nice. Corvel nodded matily to me and I almost nodded back. "Hi, Rodney," he said. He might have been picking daisies. "Shoulda told me you was round Mrs Verny's last night. I never knew you was there. That's not very nice, keeping secrets from me." The Squit was begging for mercy, his pasty cheeks streaked with tears, but I knew there wasn't a lot of the milk of human kindness flowing round just then.

I also knew I had to get it over with quickly,

so I said, "Let the kid go."

I didn't so much say it as croak it.

Corvel just stared at me.

"You gone loopy, Rodney?"

"Let him go," I said.

Corvel came out of the cubicle. Byrne laughed and slammed the door on the Squit. Corvel came straight over and started eye-balling me. Hamilton might have seen fear in those eyes, but that wasn't what I saw.

"You gone soft in the head, Rodney?" he said, standing right close.

Byrne laughed and started coming towards me; I realized now I'd made a mistake.

Just then Desmond came in. His face was whiter than the tiles behind him, and his teeth clattered like engine-wheels over a badly-made junction. "Headmaster wants to see you, Byrney," he said.

"Who says?"

"Some kid."

"When?"

"Just now."

"Something up with you, Fiely, you greasy slug?" said Corvel.

"No," said Desmond. "I'm fine."

"What kid?" asked Byrne.

"I don't know," said Desmond. "I think he's in the fourth year."

Corvel looked at me, and I tried to look suitably amazed.

"What's he want to see me for?" asked Byrne, still suspicious.

"I don't know," said Desmond. Then, after a pause, "He said something about making you a prefect."

"A prefect?" said Byrne. A glow of civic pride spread over him. His eyes went soggy and you could practically see the badge on his lapel already. He was ideal prefect material because all they did was shout at you when teachers were around, and kick you up the bum when they weren't. "I better go," he said.

"Don't!" said Corvel. "Come back!"

But Byrne had already gone. The door swung to as Desmond followed him out. The only sounds were the dripping of the cisterns and the Squit still snivelling, and – from the playground – the oblivious happy roar of kids playing.

"You can go if you like, Rodney," said Corvel.

"I don't want to go," I said.

"What's up? You out of your tiny little mind?"

"It's not me that's out of my mind," I said. "It's you that's out of yours, Corvel. You really ought to see a doctor."

"I do not believe this!" he said.

"You better," I said.

I moved away in case he kneed me – and I

swung a punch at the same time. It missed him. But it didn't matter.

He came towards me. He started explaining what he was going to do with me. Teachers think I'm hot on words, but they've never heard Corvel in full spate. He has this awfully vivid imagination which delves into all the sordid little details. He could write a story if he tried. A horror story. When he whispers at you, it's as if he's driving a spigot into your guts and then turning a tap to let them all dribble away.

I could feel that happening to me now.

We were both slinging punches but neither of us was landing a blow. We were more likely to damage the wash-basins than anything else. That was because we were both scared. And it might have gone on like that forever, if something hadn't happened.

Hamilton and all his friends came in, which they weren't supposed to. I'd told them to wait outside and stop Byrne returning. But, as it happened, it was the best thing they could have done.

The point is, I can't help responding to an audience; and the bigger the audience, the more I respond.

"What the heck's going on here?" asked Corvel.

"Just friends of mine," I said, and I whammed him in the chest.

It was a good straight left – I could see Hamilton approved – and Corvel staggered back. I don't normally go in for hitting people. In fact, I don't think I'd ever hit anyone before in my life (except Lester, of course, and he doesn't count). And after this, my first experience, I decided to abandon the idea altogether because it really hurt my knuckles. I honestly thought I'd broken at least two bones, and was about to call a truce when Corvel hurled himself at me.

We started fighting in earnest. Normally, I'm keen on boxing only if somebody else is doing it, but I was definitely winning. Cheered on by my fans, I was hitting him, first on the arms, then on the chest, then – when I felt heroic enough – on the face. And he was scared now, really scared. He was going back all the time. The Squit opened his cubicle door so he could have a ringside seat, and that increased my fighting powers even more.

I was doing very well until Byrne walked in.

THIRTY

At first I thought, *This is the end!* but for once in my life I was wrong.

The moment Byrne stepped through the door, Hamilton and his Merry Men piled on to him, followed by Lester, followed by Desmond Fiely, who took a deep breath and joined in the fray. The whole heap of them rose and fell, rose and fell, as Byrne struggled to find his feet and throw them off. It was like watching Gulliver trying to free himself from his bonds, I thought, or Giant Despair caught in a barrel of treacle, or maybe like –

And maybe that's my trouble. Maybe I think too much. Because I was still dwelling on the right words to describe the scene as I turned back to face Corvel. I hardly noticed his fist coming for my mouth.

It was the worst thing he could have done. If he'd hit any other part of my anatomy, things might have worked out differently. But – as Lester never tires of pointing out – my mouth is my biggest asset. Not only that. I tasted blood. My own blood. Anybody else's I wouldn't have minded.

I went mad. I hit him again and again, and each time I hit him, he staggered back. But it wasn't a pushover. At one point Byrne looked like breaking free, and that was an anxious moment – but Harriet came in holding aloft Hamilton's skateboard and, after a wonderfully heart-felt swing-back, she whopped Byrne with it in a place I shall not lower myself to mention.

Observing the gusto of Harriet's swing-back, and the full-blooded nature of her delivery, I realized what had been wrong with my own effort. My heart hadn't been in it. Your heart has to be in a thing if you're really going to do it well. And mine was in this now. I was hitting Corvel to make up for all the times I'd been scared, and had altered myself to fit his idea of me – pretending, looking away, watching and not seeing. And that wasn't all. I was hitting him for Mrs Verny and Charlie and Tiddles, Mrs Wright, Desmond and Harriet, for Hamilton and his Merry Men, for Lois and my little brother, even for the Squit, who had opened the door wide and was now squeaking support. I was hitting him for Charlotte, of course, but perhaps most of all, if I could have admitted it, for my dad, who all those years ago had failed to achieve what I was achieving now.

Corvel went down on the floor again and again. Eventually he didn't get up.

"Don't hit me any more, Rodney," he said.

"What did you say?"

"I'm sorry," he said.

"Get up and fight like a man!" I said. (A line from *Wholly Murder*, uttered by Smallpiece, the Reverend Staystill's surprisingly virile young curate, after he's thrashed a thug to within an inch of his life.)

A moment later, Charlotte brought in Mr Toogood.

"What exactly is going on here?" he said.

"These two boys were bullying this first year, sir," I said, "and I tried to stop them. That's all."

"On your own, Rodney?" asked Mr Toogood.

I almost said yes, but stopped myself just in time.

"We're all in this together, sir," I said. "We're a team."

"Definitely, sir," said Hamilton. "Especially me!" and he threw a straight left.

"We were just trying to help, sir," said Desmond, wiping a speck of blood – probably mine – from the end of his big nose. There was a chorus of approval from the other dwarfs.

"It was me they was bullying, sir," said the Squit, swaggering bravely from his cubicle. "They been bullying me ever since I come to this school."

"And there's something else about Corvel I want to report, sir," I said. "And I think Desmond Fiely wants to tell you something as well, sir, something they forced him to do and he wants to tell you about it before it's too late."

"Is that a fact?" said Mr Toogood, looking perkier than I'd seen him look for a day or two. (Perhaps he could see his prospects of that deputy headship improving.) "I think you'd all better come to my room."

Meanwhile, Charlotte had been watching me with her bone-melting eyes, which I have possibly mentioned before, and which one day I hope to make mine.

Naturally, I tried my best to look modest. But it wasn't easy.

THIRTY-ONE

That night, as soon as we saw Mrs DeWinter's taxi go, we bombed round to Lois's, the whole lot of us: Desmond and Harriet, Lester and Oscar, Charlotte and yours very truly.

"And now, ladies and gentlemen," said Lester as he arranged the seven candles about the room, "the world-famous defective, Hercules Porridge, will give all us dimwits a full explanation."

It wasn't exactly Colonel Clutterbuck's library, I thought. Nor was the assembled audience as polite and respectable as it ought to have been. But in this life – as opposed to a detective novel – nothing works out perfectly, and you have to make do with what you get.

"First of all, Lois," I said, "you can stop being scared of Corvel."

"Excuse me, Rodney," said Desmond. He leaned forward and coughed importantly. "I think you've made a mistake. I don't think Lois ever was scared of Corvel."

"Wasn't she?" I said.

"'Course she wasn't!" said Lester. "Have you forgotten what she did to him in the yard?"

The poor mutts still didn't understand.

"You weren't scared of Corvel to begin

with, were you, Lois?" I said. "That day in the yard when he whispered in your ear, you weren't scared at all. He may have said horrible nasty things, but he was making them up. Remember what you said? *Sticks and stones.* But last night Hamilton saw him whisper something else to you, down at the lights, something that made you turn back. Something that did frighten you."

Hamilton smiled apologetically across at her.

"Was that because he whispered the truth last night, Lois?" I asked.

She gave the slightest nod of her head.

"Was it about shoplifting?" I asked her.

"Don't spoil things, Rodney," said Charlotte. But Lois blushed and looked down.

"You needn't worry, Lois," I said. "I guess that the shoplifting Corvel found out about happened at your other school, didn't it? Corvel forced Desmond," – here, Desmond coughed uncomfortably and faded into the background – "to nosey into your files because after you knocked him down in the yard he wanted a hold over you: some kind of power. But he won't say much more about it. The police are coming to see him tomorrow. *We* know, of course – but as far as we're concerned the past is the past. We'd like you as our friend, Lois, if that's what you want?"

There was a general mumble-wumble of

approval at this point, and Charlotte beamed at me.

"All seven of us!" my little brother said. "Including Oscar!"

"Nine, actually, Lester," I said. "You're forgetting the other two dogs – which, at first, I admit, I was wrong about."

"You still could be wrong!" said Lester.

"But not in the way you think," I said. "To begin with I assumed that the motive for stealing the dogs must be a bad one, which is why I suspected Corvel. But it wasn't him."

"If it wasn't Corvel, then who was it?" asked Charlotte.

"It was Lois who took the dogs," I said. "Both of them. Am I right, or am I right?"

Lois nodded. She looked ashamed. "There's no need to look like that, Lois," I said. "Why don't you explain to us about the dogs? And about the Guides at the same time?"

Lois looked at us.

"When I was in the Guides," she said, "before I came here, we used to have these Chat and Cheer nights when we went out and talked to old ladies. I really loved them."

I nodded and smiled at her.

"I'd seen Mrs Verny plenty of times, shopping and that," she said. "That first week we came here I didn't go to school. Just explored the streets. Mum thought I was at school but I wasn't."

"Why didn't you go, Lois?" asked Harriet.

"I didn't want to," said Lois. "Simple as that."

"Had you been truanting at the other school as well?" I asked.

"That was partly it. But it wasn't the same here. I meant to go that first morning, but when I looked through the school railings everybody seemed to know everybody else. I didn't think they'd want me."

"It isn't really like that," said Charlotte.

"I know that now. But I didn't know it then. Another reason was Mum made me wear my private school uniform – she's a bit of a snob, my mum."

I guessed there was another reason why her mum had made Lois wear her old school togs, but – being my usual tactful self – I said nothing.

"Anyhow, I thought I wouldn't be noticed if I wore my old Guide outfit and called on Mrs Verny – like one of the old Chat and Cheer nights. At first that was all we did. Just chatted, had a cup of tea and that. But then the whole thing came out. She told me all about these two boys who were frightening her, asking her for money. And one night they came round when I was there."

"What happened?" I said.

"Corvel mouthed off at her on the intercom. It was horrible."

"What did he say?" asked Charlotte.

"The usual stuff. *Hello, old lady. It's your two friends come to visit you about Charlie.* Really horrible. He has a way with words. Anyhow, I told Mrs Verny not to let them in. We just sat there listening to him. He gives you the creeps. Poor Mrs Verny was shaking like a leaf. She was scared of what they'd do to Charlie. So that night I took him with me."

"In the shopping bag?" I asked.

"That's right. In case Corvel saw him. I was worried, though. The bag looked so heavy."

I smiled across at Hamilton.

"And then you got Mrs Verny to send a message to school to say Charlie was lost, so that Corvel wouldn't come round any more? And since then you've been keeping Charlie safe in your basement?"

"That's right," said Lois. "I had to keep him down there. Mum doesn't like dogs. In fact she hates them. She doesn't like any pets, really. She'd throw a hairy if she found out, and in any case, I don't think we could afford it just now."

"Especially two dogs," I said.

Lois nodded.

"It wasn't the same with Mrs Wright," she said. "That first day I walked past the school – the day I was telling you about – I saw her looking out of her window and I just felt sorry for her."

186

"I know what you mean," said Charlotte.

"I saw her two or three times after that. I used to wave to her, but she never waved back. Then last Friday night Mum and me had this really big row – she'd found out I hadn't been to school – and I put on my Guide outfit again and went round to see Mrs Wright. I needed somebody to talk to. She wasn't very nice. She kept boasting, like my dad used to. She kept telling me her niece was somebody important in the BBC. I never even knew Bess was there till she asked me to get her some coal."

"And you saw Bess at the foot of the basement steps?" I asked.

"That's right. She looked awful. Like stuck down a hole."

"Like the Black Hole of Calcutta," said Lester.

"Right," said Lois, smiling at him.

"But you didn't take her that night?" I asked.

"No. I just took her for a romp in the garden, that's all. Her legs were stiff with cold. She could hardly walk. I took her on Saturday night. There were two reasons. First there was a downpour that night. I kept thinking of her getting soaked. Second, Charlie was getting lonely and the weather was turning cold. I thought she might keep Charlie company – and keep him warm because she's big and fluffy. I intended taking her back before Mrs Wright's niece came back on the following

Friday. That's why I nearly passed out last night at Mrs Verny's, when you said she'd come early."

"I guessed that," I said. "And you'd told Mrs Verny about the niece, hadn't you?"

"Yes," said Lois.

"Do try to stop boasting, Rodney," said Charlotte.

"He can't help it," Lester told her.

"Then on Monday night," said Lois, "I had the dogs in our back garden and I saw you coming over the fence from Mrs Wright's. I wondered what you were up to. I thought maybe you were on my trail, so I crept as close to your shed as I could, to listen. I must have stood on a stick or something. I was scared to death when you came after me. I thought you'd find out about the dogs and everything and tell my mum. I was just round the corner of the house with them both, when you came into our garden."

"And who was it we saw in the cellar?" I said. "The new vicar?"

"That's right. Mr Speedwell – Arthur. He doesn't like being called Reverend. He says it's old-fashioned. He'd been helping to clear a load of old bottles that the people before us had left in the basement. I didn't want the dogs to get hurt with broken glass. Arthur promised not to tell my mum for a week."

"These dogs been out tonight?" asked Hamilton.

"Not yet. I usually take them out after Mum's gone to work."

"What's she do?" asked Charlotte.

"Organizes posh dinner parties for people."

"Can we take the dogs out for a romp now?" asked Harriet.

"Why not?" said Lois.

"So how much did you overhear that night?" I asked her as we gathered up the candles.

"Not a lot," said Lois. "I was just relieved when I heard you suspected somebody else. I was in enough trouble already. By then I'd stolen the cat food as well."

"Was that the same night you took Charlie?"

"Yes. I deliberately left his red blanket, so Corvel would believe he was lost, but I forgot his food. I didn't want to bother Mrs Verny – I knew she didn't have any money anyhow – so I just nicked it. I never told Mrs Verny. Then when Charlotte told me you'd stopped suspecting Corvel, I thought I'd better join you, in case you were on to me."

"I thought as much," I said.

"Rodney!" said Charlotte.

"Also," Lois said as we descended the basement steps, "I wanted you to find out about Corvel and Mrs Verny – what he was up to."

The dogs had started barking as Lois unlocked the door. Charlie rushed about, trying to lick everyone's hand at once. Lois went straight up to Bess and began to speak to her. You could see at once that there was something special between those two.

We took the dogs up into the garden. It was a lovely starry night. Charlie romped with Hamilton and my little brother – there's nothing quite like watching young animals at play. Lois walked quietly up the garden, Bess by her side. Oscar surveyed the whole happy scene as if he was personally responsible!

Beyond Lois and Bess I could see the lit-up windows of Mrs Wright's kitchen. She was at the sink, probably making herself a lonely cup of tea before settling down to watch the News. Standing by that window, looking out, she had no idea what was going on here, under the stars – right under her nose, as you might say. Which was sad.

I made up my mind to go and see Mrs Wright. I was tiring of my detective phase, but if nothing else, the last few days had shown me how lonely some old people could be; and not only *old* people.

"They're made for one another, those two," said Charlotte, meaning Lois and Bess, who were now at the top end of the garden. "Lois is going to miss that dog when she goes."

"She'll still have Charlie and Oscar," I said.

"And Mrs Verny. And us. Besides, when she takes Bess back tomorrow night she might make another friend."

"How do you mean, Rodney?"

"Mrs Wright's niece," I said. "She's another one who's lonely."

Charlotte looked at me.

"I didn't know you'd noticed that, Rodney," she said.

I didn't answer. I pretended to be engrossed in the stars.

It's amazing how many people underestimate me.

THIRTY-TWO

The Vista Hill Spillage was front-page news for two days. Some people had to be evacuated from their homes, and there was plenty of bilge spouted about Britain's Old Wartime Spirit. In Parliament, the opposition brayed like a herd of demented donkeys for a whole week. The government, which said it had no intention whatsoever of resigning, resigned shortly afterwards.

It took longer than that for Mrs DeWinter to get her electricity switched back on. But there is light now at number eleven, I'm glad to say, and furniture – awful trendy stuff – has recently started materializing all over the house. Lois told us last night that her mum had just been made something big in the up-market catering firm she works for. Any day now another Jag will haul itself on to the front gravel to lie basking in the sun.

I realize that Mrs DeWinter isn't everybody's cup of perfect mum, but there's something about her... When your husband leaves you, when you have to organize dinner parties instead of giving your own, when your life falls apart and you can't pay the bills, you need courage to start again. I have only to look at

Mrs DeWinter to know where Lois gets hers from. I think even Lois is beginning to appreciate that now.

And it was Lois, of course, who first showed me the way when she stood up to Corvel in the yard.

He's much quieter now. You wouldn't recognize him. His mum and dad were shocked when he had to go in front of the magistrates. I don't think they'd ever realized. He still smiles occasionally, but he isn't the same kid at all – especially since Byrne became a regular member of the soccer team and now expends his brute force more legitimately.

Now and again, when Corvel revives his old habits, kids holler for me because they know I'm the tough guy of the school – and I must say it's nice to know my talents are recognized. Like Dad's: his final Staystill novel – *The Case of the Crazy Chiropodist* – was given a top award by the Detective Writers' Club. (Not all his titles are this corny, by the way.)

Even *he*'s changed. He's joined Mum's protest group, and after writing sixteen detective stories in a row, ending up with that winner, he's now switched to writing science fiction instead – don't ask me why.

We all keep an eye on Mrs Verny. She's happier now. Hamilton's brother turned his amplifiers down as soon as we mentioned the noise, and now you can only just hear them from

Birmingham. He always winks at me when I see him pounding the beat, and I often wonder if he's still wearing the same T-shirt beneath the regulation blue.

As I predicted, Lois and Sally Bright get on well together. We often see them taking Bess for a walk. They look happier. Maybe Bess has something to do with that. Mrs Wright, though, hasn't changed at all. She doesn't approve of the vicar wearing an old greatcoat and jeans – some people are so prejudiced about the clothes people wear, don't you think? – and she still hasn't offered us a piece of cake. We often call to see her and we stay until I can't bear it any longer: she keeps telling us what a godsend her husband was to the borough council. Oh dear.

"What is the point of going round at all?" I often ask Charlotte.

"You have to keep trying, Rodney," she says. "Everything changes."

She could be right. Perhaps one day we *shall* be offered some cake.

I've certainly changed. Though I suppose that's nothing new.

Three things convinced me I was not cut out for the detective game. The first was when I woke up and realized I'd detected myself into real trouble. I'd started off meaning to go for a paddle and ended up swimming for my life. The second was later, when I hit Corvel. It really hurt my knuckles. I don't think I mentioned it at the time, because I'm like that – the sort who suffers in silence – but if there's one thing I can't stand it's pain. And there seemed to be a lot of pain in the detective business. The third reason was that Mr Battrey's engagement to Miss Byeline was announced near the end of the term.

"Didn't you know about it?" Charlotte asked me.

"Even I knew about that," said Lois. "I guessed the first day I saw them together in the dining-hall – the way she blushed."

"I thought everybody knew," said my little brother.

"You mean there was some mutt who didn't?" asked Hamilton the Third.

That was the day I finally ditched the idea of being a detective.

The following day, I caught up Miss Quibble on the way to assembly and told her I'd decided to sacrifice myself to the mag. It seemed only sensible, really. There were other people in our school who could write, of course. But none of them as brilliant as me.

"Good!" Miss Quibble said. "Mr Toogood and I were discussing it only last night, and we decided it might be an idea if you started with a really nice long story."

"How long, miss?"

"Say thirty-two chapters?"

"Why thirty-two?"

"It's a nice round number."

"You're sure you don't want anything longer?" I asked.

"Best to start modestly, Rodney," she said.

"He always is modest, miss!" said Charlotte, catching up with us.

"What sort of a story?" I asked Miss Quibble.

"I thought a detective story might be nice?"

"Did you say a de*fec*tive story, miss?" asked my little brother, joggling up like a lump of jetsam.

"Brilliant idea, Lester!" she said. "Why don't you make it a story about a defective detective, Rodney? That could give it an edge."

"To be honest, miss, I'm heavily into dogs at the moment," I said, "and I wouldn't have a clue about writing a detective story."

"You really are so witty, Rodney," she said. "Why don't you make it a comic detective story about a defective detective hunting a dog?"

"Or dogs, miss," suggested my little brother.

"Even better!"

"But how should I start?" I asked.

"If I were you, Rodney," she said with a sly smile, "I should start by going into assembly!"

And, believe it or not, that's exactly what I did.

P.S. You haven't forgotten about Miss Airey's waterproof compass, have you? It was in the hamster cage all the time. Harriet Farlaughn must have dropped it in there when she was feeding the hamster. I'm pleased, in a way, that my little brother was right about one thing.

RIDE ON, SISTER VINCENT
by Dyan Sheldon

"A miracle. That's what St Agnes really needs. A miracle, not a motor mechanic."

Sent to the dilapidated convent school, St Agnes in the Pasture, dynamic, globe-trotting Sister Vincent, teacher of motor mechanics, feels like a fish out of water. Certainly Mother Margaret Aloysius, the nuns and the school's three young pupils consider her a bit of an odd fish. The Lord, it seems, is moving in a very mysterious way indeed – until a discovery in the old barn enables Sister Vincent to give the run-down school a surprising and exhilarating kick-start!

NOT JUST JEMIMA

Sally Christie

*"God, you're stupid, Tamsin Langridge.
You and your stupid goat!"*

Tamsin is in her first term at Swinston
Secondary School – and she hates it.
Teachers, lessons, children ... she can't
seem to get on with any of them even her
friends from primary school. Then she
makes a new and very special friend –
Jemima.

"When a tale appears that is truly about
the condition of being young – all the
disgrace and dismay and confusing
excitement of it – it's time to cheer... Such
a good writer while still young, Sally
Christie is going to be a marvellous writer
before long."
Edward Blishen, The Evening Standard

Shortlisted for the
Writers' Guild Children's Book Award

THE BEAST OF WHIXALL MOSS
by Pauline Fisk

"He watched the beast run ahead of them, shining, leaping, bounding. He didn't ever want to be lonely again. He didn't ever want to let the beast go."

At the age of eleven, Jack is resigned to his world. So what if he can never match up to his mother's desire for perfection, and his brother can? So what if it's lonely out on Whixall Moss, with nobody living nearby and nothing to do? He doesn't care, or so he likes to tell himself. Then one day Jack finds a boat hidden on the creek – and in the boat a fabulous beast. At once he is filled with a wild longing: he must own it. But the mysterious inhabitants of the boat have other ideas, and in the struggles that follow, Jack's world is changed for ever.

Gripping and powerful, Smarties Book Prize Winner Pauline Fisk's novel is a tale that will live long in the imagination.

JOHNNY CASANOVA
by Jamie Rix

Johnny Worms is hot to trot, the unstoppable sex machine, Johnny Casanova... Well, so he believes. So when love's thunderbolt strikes in the form of Alison Mallinson or a beautiful vision in purple what can Johnny do? And is it his fault that Cyborg Girl, Deborah Smeeton, finds him irresistible?

"A genuinely funny book, sparklingly well-written." *The Independent*

"The first chapter had me laughing aloud at least three times." *The Scotsman*

THE ROPE SCHOOL
by Sam Llewellyn

"Far out there on the knife-cut rim of the world, a tiny sun winked and died...

Kate said, 'What—'

Jago turned. 'Breathe a word,' he said. 'One word. And I'll kill ye.'"

It's 1813 and England is at war with France and America. Entirely by accident, eleven-year-old Kate Griffiths finds herself disguised as a boy, at sea on one of His Majesty's sloops of war. Under the watchful eye of the mysterious Jago, Kate learns about hammock hook hitches and sheet bends, shrouds and sails, as well as the often harsh reality of shipboard life. But this is nothing to the tangled knot of mystery and adventure that awaits her on the high seas!

THE TIME TREE

Enid Richemont

Rachel and Joanna are best friends and the tall tree in the park is their special place. It's Anne's too. So it hardly seems surprising that the three girls meet up there – except for the fact that four centuries divide their lives.

"Ms Richemont develops her story beautifully, with finely controlled writing and clear delineation of her three main characters."
The Junior Bookshelf

THE LIFE AND LOVES OF
ZOË T. CURLEY
by Martin Waddell

"For a whole month I am going to write something every day about Zoë T. Curley: her Life and Loves. This is part of my training to be a Famous Writer."

It's not easy being an aspiring teenager with a brace and the body of a "fat elephant". This is the lot of Zoë T. Curley, sister of Ob-Noxious and Creep, and prisoner of Zog, the life system invented by Zoë's temperamental writer father (alias The Creative) to keep order in the Curley household. Fortunately, Zoë has a loyal best friend, Melissa, with whom she can discuss – at length – her many domestic woes, as well as such vital matters as her proposed Sky Cabin, the scandalous goings-on with the Bluebottles next door, the treachery of Awful Alison and Sneaky Sonja from the tennis club, and, of course, BOYS and LOVE. Follow the fluctuating fortunes of our ear-wiggling heroine throughout one turbulent month in this entertaining and keenly observed diary novel by double Smarties Book Prize Winner, Martin Waddell.

NORMAL NESBITT, THE ABNORMALLY AVERAGE BOY
by Nick Warburton

"I am average. I am dull. I'm not surprised people can't remember my name. I'm so dull I'm afraid I might forget it myself."

Meet Gordon Nesbitt, The Average Pupil. That's what the computer says, anyway, and no one will let him forget it. In fact, to Nesbitt's increasing dismay, his normality seems to be attracting an abnormal degree of interest – even his dog gets in on the act. But when the gorgeous new girl, the Dumb Blonde, joins in, Nesbitt is moved to action – with quite extraordinary results!

"Very well done ... there's much humour and many witty scenes." *Books For Keeps*

"Hilarious." *The Daily Telegraph*

THE BATTLE OF
BAKED BEAN ALLEY
by Nick Warburton

Well, I went down the Green
And what did I see, waitin' for to
* meet my eyes?*
A dirty great fence was what I
* done se-en,*
A-blockin' me off from my prize...

Ivor Demetrius is angy – and he's written a
protest song to prove it. Turnovers, the local
mega-market, wants to build a baked bean
extension on Ivor's local green, cutting down
his beloved oak tree in the process.
Unfortunately, Ivor's song – his whole cam-
paign, in fact – seems to be falling on deaf ears.
There's nothing for it but to go to the top –
Lady Blitherwicke. First, though, he has to get
past her villainous butler, Stote, and his cronies
... and that's when the real battle begins!